THE HOLY DOOR

and other stories

Frank O'Connor was born in Cork in 1903. He had no formal education worth speaking of and his only real ambition was to become a writer. At the age of twelve he began to prepare a collected edition of his own works and, having learnt to speak Gaelic while very young, he studied his native poetry, music and legends. His literary career began with the translation of one of du Bellay's sonnets into Gaelic.

On release from imprisonment by the Free State Government for his part in the Civil War, O'Connor won a prize for his study of Turgenev, and subsequently had poetry, stories and translations published in the *Irish Statesman*. He caused great consternation in his native city by producing plays by Ibsen and Chekhov: a local clergyman remarked that the producer 'would go down in posterity at the head of the Pagan Dublin muses', and ladies in the local literary society threatened to resign when he mentioned the name of James Joyce.

O'Connor's other great interest was music, Mozart and the Irish composer Carolan being his favourites. By profession he was a librarian. He died in 1966 and will be long remembered as one of the great masters of short story writing.

THE HOLY DOOR
and other stories

FRANK O'CONNOR

Selected by Harriet Sheehy

PAN BOOKS LTD : LONDON

This collection selected from *The Stories of Frank O'Connor*,
first published in Great Britain 1953 by Hamish Hamilton Ltd,
and *Domestic Relations*, first published in Great Britain 1957
by Hamish Hamilton Ltd.
This edition published 1973 by Pan Books Ltd,
33 Tothill Street, London SW1

ISBN 0 330 23557 5

*Printed and bound in England by
Hazell Watson & Viney Ltd,
Aylesbury, Bucks*

The following stories were printed – some of them in somewhat different form – in earlier collections of Frank O'Connor's stories: 'Old Fellows' and 'The House that Johnny Built' in *Crab Apple Jelly*; and 'News for the Church', 'The Holy Door' and 'The Babes in the Wood' in *The Common Chord*. 'A Bachelor's Story' appeared originally in the *New Yorker* and 'Orphans' in *Mademoiselle*.

CONTENTS

Christmas Morning

I never really liked my brother, Sonny. From the time he was a baby he was always the mother's pet and always chasing her to tell her what mischief I was up to. Mind you, I was usually up to something. Until I was nine or ten I was never much good at school, and I really believe it was to spite me that he was so smart at his books. He seemed to know by instinct that this was what Mother had set her heart on, and you might almost say he spelt himself into her favour.

'Mummy,' he'd say, 'will I call Larry in to his t-e-a?' or: 'Mummy, the k-e-t-e-l is boiling,' and, of course, when he was wrong she'd correct him, and next time he'd have it right and there would be no standing him. 'Mummy,' he'd say, 'aren't I a good speller?' Cripes, we could all be good spellers if we went on like that!

Mind you, it wasn't that I was stupid. Far from it. I was just restless and not able to fix my mind for long on any one thing. I'd do the lessons for the year before, or the lessons for the year after: what I couldn't stand were the lessons we were supposed to be doing at the time. In the evenings I used to go out and play with the Doherty gang. Not, again, that I was rough, but I liked the excitement, and for the life of me I couldn't see what attracted Mother about education.

'Can't you do your lessons first and play after?' she'd say, getting white with indignation. 'You ought to be ashamed of yourself that your baby brother can read better than you.'

She didn't seem to understand that I wasn't, because there didn't seem to me to be anything particularly praiseworthy about reading, and it struck me as an occupation better suited to a sissy kid like Sonny.

'The dear knows what will become of you,' she'd say. 'If only you'd stick to your books you might be something good like a clerk or an engineer.'

'I'll be a clerk, Mummy,' Sonny would say smugly.

'Who wants to be an old clerk?' I'd say, just to annoy him. 'I'm going to be a soldier.'

'The dear knows, I'm afraid that's all you'll ever be fit for,' she would add with a sigh.

I couldn't help feeling at times that she wasn't all there. As if there was anything better a fellow could be!

Coming on to Christmas, with the days getting shorter and the shopping crowds bigger, I began to think of all the things I might get from Santa Claus. The Dohertys said there was no Santa Claus, only what your father and mother gave you, but the Dohertys were a rough class of children you wouldn't expect Santa to come to anyway. I was rooting round for whatever information I could pick up about him, but there didn't seem to be much. I was no hand with a pen, but if a letter would do any good I was ready to chance writing to him. I had plenty of initiative and was always writing off for free samples and prospectuses.

'Ah, I don't know will he come at all this year,' Mother said with a worried air. 'He has enough to do looking after steady boys who mind their lessons without bothering about the rest.'

'He only comes to good spellers, Mummy,' said Sonny. 'Isn't that right?'

'He comes to any little boy who does his best, whether he's a good speller or not,' Mother said firmly.

Well, I did my best. God knows I did! It wasn't my fault if, four days before the holidays, Flogger Dawley gave us sums we couldn't do, and Peter Doherty and myself had to go on the lang. It wasn't for the love of it, for, take it from me, December is no month for mitching, and we spent most of our time sheltering from the rain in a store on the quays. The only mistake we made was imagining we could keep it up till the holidays without being spotted. That showed real lack of foresight.

Of course, Flogger Dawley noticed and sent home word to know what was keeping me. When I came in on the third day the mother gave me a look I'll never forget, and said: 'Your dinner is there.' She was too full to talk. When I tried to explain to her about Flogger Dawley and the sums she brushed it aside and said: 'You have no word.' I saw then it wasn't the langing she minded but the lies, though I still didn't see how you could lang without lying. She didn't speak to me for days. And even then I couldn't make out what she saw in education, or why she wouldn't let me grow up naturally like anyone else.

To make things worse, it stuffed Sonny up more than ever. He had the air of one saying: 'I don't know what they'd do without me in this blooming house.' He stood at the front door, leaning against the jamb with his hands in his trouser pockets, trying to make himself look like Father, and shouted to the other kids so that he could be heard all over the road.

'Larry isn't left go out. He went on the lang with Peter Doherty and me mother isn't talking to him.'

And at night, when we were in bed, he kept it up.

'Santa Claus won't bring you anything this year, aha!'

'Of course he will,' I said.

'How do you know?'

'Why wouldn't he?'

'Because you went on the lang with Doherty. I wouldn't play with them Doherty fellows.'

'You wouldn't be left.'

'I wouldn't play with them. They're no class. They had the bobbies up to the house.'

'And how would Santa know I was on the lang with Peter Doherty?' I growled, losing patience with the little prig.

'Of course he'd know. Mummy would tell him.'

'And how could Mummy tell him and he up at the North Pole? Poor Ireland, she's rearing them yet! 'Tis easy seen you're only an old baby.'

'I'm not a baby, and I can spell better than you, and Santa won't bring you anything.'

'We'll see whether he will or not,' I said sarcastically, doing the old man on him.

But, to tell the God's truth, the old man was only bluff. You could never tell what powers these superhuman chaps would have of knowing what you were up to. And I had a bad conscience about the langing because I'd never before seen the mother like that.

That was the night I decided that the only sensible thing to do was to see Santa myself and explain to him. Being a man, he'd probably understand. In those days I was a good-looking kid and had a way with me when I liked. I had only to smile nicely at one old gent on the North Mall to get a penny from him, and I felt if only I could get Santa by himself I could do the same with him and maybe get something worthwhile from him. I wanted a model railway: I was sick of Ludo and Snakes-and-Ladders.

I started to practise lying awake, counting five hundred and then a thousand, and trying to hear first eleven, then midnight, from Shandon. I felt sure Santa would be round by midnight, seeing that he'd be coming from the north, and would have the whole of the south side to do afterwards. In some ways I was very farsighted. The only trouble was the things I was farsighted about.

I was so wrapped up in my own calculations that I had little attention to spare for Mother's difficulties. Sonny and I used to go to town with her, and while she was shopping we stood outside a toyshop in the North Main Street, arguing about what we'd like for Christmas.

On Christmas Eve when Father came home from work and gave her the housekeeping money, she stood looking at it doubtfully while her face grew white.

'Well?' he snapped, getting angry. 'What's wrong with that?'

'What's wrong with it?' she muttered. 'On Christmas Eve!'

'Well,' he asked truculently, sticking his hands in his trouser pockets as though to guard what was left, 'do you think I get more because it's Christmas?'

'Lord God,' she muttered distractedly. 'And not a bit of cake in the house, nor a candle, nor anything!'

'All right,' he shouted, beginning to stamp. 'How much will the candle be?'

'Ah, for pity's sake,' she cried, 'will you give me the money and not argue like that before the children? Do you think I'll leave them with nothing on the one day of the year?'

'Bad luck to you and your children!' he snarled. 'Am I to be slaving from one year's end to another for you to be throwing it away on toys? Here,' he added, tossing two half-crowns on the table, 'that's all you're going to get, so make the most of it.'

'I suppose the publicans will get the rest,' she said bitterly.

Later she went into town, but did not bring us with her, and returned with a lot of parcels, including the Christmas candle. We waited for Father to come home to his tea, but he didn't, so we had our own tea and a slice of Christmas cake each, and then Mother put Sonny on a chair with the holy-water stoup to sprinkle the candle, and when he lit it she said: 'The light of heaven to our souls.' I could see she was upset because Father wasn't in – it should be the oldest and youngest. When we hung up our stockings at bedtime he was still out.

Then began the hardest couple of hours I ever put in. I was mad with sleep but afraid of losing the model railway, so I lay for a while, making up things to say to Santa when he came. They varied in tone from frivolous to grave, for some old gents like kids to be modest and well spoken, while others prefer them with spirit. When I had rehearsed them all I tried to wake Sonny to keep me company, but that kid slept like the dead.

Eleven struck from Shandon, and soon after I heard the latch, but it was only Father coming home.

'Hello, little girl,' he said, letting on to be surprised at finding Mother waiting for him, and then broke into a self-conscious giggle. 'What have you up so late?'

'Do you want your supper?' she asked shortly.

'Ah, no, no,' he replied. 'I had a bit of pig's cheek at Daneen's on my way up.' (Daneen was my uncle.) 'I'm very fond of a bit of pig's cheek ... My goodness, is it that late?' he exclaimed, letting on to be astonished. 'If I knew that I'd have gone to the North Chapel for midnight Mass. I'd like to hear the *Adeste* again. That's a hymn I'm very fond of – a most touching hymn.'

Then he began to hum it falsetto.

Adeste fideles
Solus domus dagus.

Father was very fond of Latin hymns, particularly when he had a drop in, but as he had no notion of the words he made them up as he went along, and this always drove Mother mad.

'Ah, you disgust me!' she said in a scalded voice, and closed the room door behind her. Father laughed as if he thought it a great joke; and he struck a match to light his pipe and for a while puffed at it noisily. The light under the door dimmed and went out but he continued to sing emotionally.

Dixie medearo
Tutum tonum tantum
Venite adoremus.

He had it all wrong but the effect was the same on me. To save my life I couldn't keep awake.

Coming on to dawn, I woke with the feeling that something dreadful had happened. The whole house was quiet, and the little bedroom that looked out on the foot and a half of back yard was pitch-dark. It was only when I glanced at the window that I saw how all the silver had drained out of the sky. I jumped out of bed to feel my stocking, well knowing that the worst had happened. Santa had come while I was asleep, and gone away with an entirely false impression of me, because all he had left me was some sort of book, folded up, a pen and pencil, and a tuppenny bag of sweets. Not even Snakes-and-Ladders! For a while I was too stunned even to think. A fellow who was able to drive over rooftops and climb down chimneys without getting stuck – God, wouldn't you think he'd know better?

Then I began to wonder what that foxy boy, Sonny, had. I went to his side of the bed and felt his stocking. For all his spelling and sucking-up he hadn't done so much better, because, apart from a bag of sweets like mine, all Santa had left him was a popgun, one that fired a cork on a piece of string and which you could get in any huxter's shop for sixpence.

All the same, the fact remained that it was a gun, and a gun was better than a book any day of the week. The Dohertys had a gang, and the gang fought the Strawberry Lane kids who tried to play football on our road. That gun would be very useful to me in many ways, while it would be lost on Sonny who wouldn't be let play with the gang, even if he wanted to.

Then I got the inspiration, as it seemed to me, direct from heaven. Suppose I took the gun and gave Sonny the book! Sonny would never be any good in the gang: he was fond of spelling, and a studious child like him could learn a lot of spellings from a book like mine. As he hadn't seen Santa any more than I had, what he hadn't seen wouldn't grieve him. I was doing no harm to anyone; in fact, if Sonny only knew, I was doing him a good turn which he might have cause to thank me for later. That was one thing I was always keen on; doing good turns. Perhaps this was Santa's intention the whole time and he had merely become confused between us. It was a mistake that might happen to anyone. So I put the book, the pencil, and the pen into Sonny's stocking and the popgun into my own, and returned to bed and slept again. As I say, in those days I had plenty of initiative.

It was Sonny who woke me, shaking me to tell me that Santa had come and left me a gun. I let on to be surprised and rather disappointed in the gun, and to divert his mind from it made him show me his picture book, and cracked it up to the skies.

As I knew, that kid was prepared to believe anything, and nothing would do him then but to take the presents in to show Father and Mother. This was a bad moment for me. After the way she had behaved about the langing, I distrusted Mother, though I had the consolation of believing that the only person who could contradict me was now somewhere up by the North Pole. That gave me a certain confidence, so Sonny and I burst in with our presents, shouting: 'Look what Santa Claus brought!'

Father and Mother woke, and Mother smiled, but only for an instant. As she looked at me her face changed. I knew that look; I knew it only too well. It was the same she had worn the day I came home from langing, when she said I had no word.

'Larry,' she said in a low voice, 'where did you get that gun?'

'Santa left it in my stocking, Mummy,' I said, trying to put on an injured air, though it baffled me how she guessed that he hadn't. 'He did, honest.'

'You stole it from that poor child's stocking while he was asleep,' she said, her voice quivering with indignation. 'Larry, Larry, how could you be so mean?'

'Now, now, now,' Father said deprecatingly, ''tis Christmas morning.'

'Ah,' she said with real passion, 'it's easy it comes to you. Do you think I want my son to grow up a liar and a thief?'

'Ah, what thief, woman?' he said testily. 'Have sense, can't you?' He was as cross if you interrupted him in his benevolent moods as if they were of the other sort, and this one was probably exacerbated by a feeling of guilt for his behaviour of the night before. 'Here, Larry,' he said, reaching out for the money on the bedside table, 'here's sixpence for you and one for Sonny. Mind you don't lose it now!'

But I looked at Mother and saw what was in her eyes. I burst out crying, threw the popgun on the floor, and ran bawling out of the house before anyone on the road was awake. I rushed up the lane beside the house and threw myself on the wet grass.

I understood it all, and it was almost more than I could bear; that there was no Santa Claus, as the Dohertys said, only Mother trying to scrape together a few coppers from the housekeeping; that Father was mean and common and a drunkard, and that she had been relying on me to raise her out of the misery of the life she was leading. And I knew that the look in her eyes was the fear that, like my father, I should turn out to be mean and common and a drunkard.

Old Fellows

If there was one thing I could not stand as a kid it was being taken out for the day by Father. My mature view is that he couldn't stand it either but did it to keep Mother quiet. Mother did it to keep him out of harm's way; I was supposed to act as a brake on him.

He always took me to the same place – Crosshaven – on the paddle-boat. He raved about Cork Harbour, its wonderful scenery and sea air. I was never one for scenery myself, and as for air, a little went a long way with me. With a man as un-observant as Father, buttons like mine, and strange boats and public-houses which I couldn't find my way about, I lived in mortal fear of an accident.

One day in particular is always in my memory; a Sunday morning with the bells ringing for Mass and the usual scramble on to get Father out of the house. He was standing before the mirror which hung over the mantelpiece, dragging madly at his dickey, and Mother on a low stool in front of him, trying to fasten the studs.

'Ah, go easy!' she said impatiently. 'Go easy, can't you?'

Father couldn't go easy. He lowered his head all right, but he shivered and reared like a bucking bronco.

'God Almighty give me patience!' he hissed between his teeth. 'Give me patience, sweet God, before I tear the bloody house down!'

It was never what you'd call a good beginning to the day. And to see him later, going down to Pope's Quay to Mass, you'd swear butter wouldn't melt in the old devil's mouth.

After Mass, as we were standing on the quay, J. J. came along. J. J. and Father were lifelong friends. He was a melancholy, reedy man with a long sallow face and big hollows under his cheeks. Whenever he was thinking deeply he sucked in the cheeks till his face caved in suddenly like a sandpit. We sauntered down a side street from the quay. I knew well where we were bound for, but with the incurable optimism of childhood I hoped again that this time we might be going somewhere else. We weren't. J. J. stopped by a door at a street corner and knocked softly. He had one ear cocked to the door and the other eye cocked at Father. A voice spoke within, a soft voice as in a confessional, and J. J. bowed his head reverently to the keyhole and whispered something back. Father raised his head with a smile and held up two fingers.

'Two minutes now!' he said, and then took a penny from his trouser pocket.

'There's a penny for you,' he said benignly. 'Mind now and be a good boy.'

The door opened and shut almost silently behind Father and J. J. I stood and looked round. The streets were almost deserted, and so silent you could hear the footsteps of people you couldn't see in the laneways high up the hill. The only living thing near me was a girl standing a little up from the street corner. She was wearing a frilly white hat and a white satiny dress. As it happened, I was wearing a sailor suit for the first time that day. It gave me a slightly raffish feeling. I went up to where she was standing, partly to see what she was looking at, partly to study her closer. She was a beautiful child – upon my word, a beautiful child! And, whatever way it happened, I smiled at her. Mind you, I didn't mean any harm. It was pure good nature. To this day, that is the sort I am, wanting to be friends with everybody.

The little girl looked at me. She looked at me for a long time; long enough at any rate for the smile to wither off me, and then drew herself up with her head in the air and walked past me down the pavement. Looking back on it, I suppose she was upset because her own father was inside the pub, and a thing like that would mean more to a girl than a boy. But it wasn't only that. By nature she was haughty and cold. It was the first time I had come face to face with the heartlessness of real beauty, and her contemptuous stare knocked me flat. I was a sensitive child. I didn't know where to look, and I wished myself back at home with my mother.

After about ten minutes Father came out with his face all shiny and I ran up to him and took his hand. Unobservant and all as he was, he must have noticed I was upset, because he was suddenly full of palaver about the grand day we were going to have by the seaside. Of course it was all propaganda, because before we reached the boat at all, he had another call.

'Two minutes now!' he said with his two fingers raised and a roguish grin on his face. 'Definitely not more than two minutes! Be a good boy!'

At last we did get aboard the paddle-steamer, and, as we moved off down the river, people stood and waved from the road at Tivoli and from under the trees on the Marina walk, while the band played on deck. It was quite exciting, really. And then, all of a sudden, I saw coming up the deck towards us the little girl who had snubbed me outside the public-house. Her father was along with her, a small, fat, red-faced man with a big black beard and a bowler hat. He walked with a sort of roll, and under his arm he carried a model ship with masts and sails – a really superior-looking ship which took my eye at once.

When my father saw him he gave a loud triumphant crow.

'We'll meet in heaven,' he said.

'I'd be surprised,' said the fat man none too pleasantly.

'Back to the old ship, I see?' said Father, giving J. J. a wink to show he could now expect some sport.

'What exactly do you mean by that?' asked the fat man, giving his moustache a twirl.

'My goodness,' said Father, letting on to be surprised, 'didn't you tell me 'twas aboard the paddle-boat in Cork Harbour you did your sailoring? Didn't you tell me yourself about the terrible storm that nearly wrecked ye between Aghada and Queenstown?'

'If I mentioned such a thing,' said the fat man, 'it was only in dread you mightn't have heard of any other place. You were never in Odessa, I suppose?'

'I had a cousin there,' said Father gravely. 'Cold, I believe. He was telling me they had to chop off the drinks with a hatchet.'

'You hadn't a cousin in Valparaiso, by any chance?'

'Well, no, now,' said Father regretfully, 'that cousin died young of a Maltese fever he contracted while he was with Nansen at the North Pole.'

'Maltese fever!' snorted the fat man. 'I suppose you couldn't even tell me where Malta is.'

By this time there was no holding the pair of them. The fat man was a sailor, and whatever the reason was, my father couldn't see a sailor without wanting to be at his throat. They went into the saloon, and all the way down the river they never as much as stuck their noses out. When I looked in, half the bar had already joined in the argument, some in favour of going to sea and some, like Father, dead against it.

'It broadens the mind, I tell you,' said the sailor. 'Sailors see the world.'

'Do they, indeed—' said Father sarcastically.

'Malta,' said the sailor. 'You were talking about Malta. Now, there's a beautiful place. The heat of the day drives off the cold of the night.'

'Do it?' asked Father in a far-away voice, gazing out the door as though he expected someone to walk in. 'Anything else?'

'San Francisco,' said the sailor dreamily, 'and the scent of the orange blossoms in the moonlight.'

'Anything else?' Father asked remorselessly. He was like a priest in the confessional.

'As much more as you fancy,' said the sailor.

'But do they see what's under their very noses?' asked Father, rising with his eyes aglow. 'Do they see their own country? Do they see that river outside that people come thousands of miles to see? What old nonsense you have!'

I looked round and saw the little girl at my elbow.

'They're at it still,' I said.

' 'Tis all your fault,' she said coldly.

'How is it my fault?'

'You and your old fellow,' she said contemptuously. 'Ye have my day ruined on me.'

And away she walked again with her head in the air.

I didn't see her again until we landed, and by that time her
father and mine had to be separated. They were on to politics,
and J. J. thought it safer to get Father away. Father was all for
William O'Brien, and he got very savage when he was contradicted. I watched the sailor and the little girl go off along the
sea-road while we went in the opposite direction. Father was
still simmering about things the sailor had said in favour of
John Redmond, a politician he couldn't like. He suddenly
stopped and raised his fists in the air.

'I declare to my God if there's one class of men I can't stand,
'tis sailors,' he said.

'They're all old blow,' agreed J. J. peaceably.

'I wouldn't mind the blooming blow,' Father said venomously. ' 'Tis all the lies they tell you. San Francisco? That
fellow was never near San Francisco. Now, I'm going back,' he
went on, beginning to stamp from one foot to the other, 'and
I'm going to tell *him* a few lies for a change.'

'I wouldn't be bothered,' said J. J., and, leaning his head
over Father's shoulder, he began to whisper in his ear the way
you'd whisper to a restive young horse, and with the same sort
of result, for Father gradually ceased his stamping and rearing
and looked doubtfully at J. J. out of the corner of his eye. A
moment later up went the two fingers.

'Two minutes,' he said with a smile that was only put on.
'Not more. Be a good boy now.'

He slipped me another copper and I sat on the sea-wall,
watching the crowds and wondering if we'd ever get out of the
village that day. Beyond the village were the cliffs, and path-
ways wound over them, in and out of groups of thatched cot-
tages. The band would be playing up there, and people would
be dancing. There would be stalls for lemonade and sweets. If
only I could get up there I should at least have something to
look at. My heart gave a jump and then sank. I saw, coming
through the crowd, the sailor and the little girl. She was swinging out of his arm, and in her own free arm she carried the
model ship. They stopped before the pub.

'Daddy,' I heard her say in that precise, ladylike little voice
of hers, 'you promised to sail my boat for me.'

'In one second now,' said her father. 'I have a certain thing to say to a man in here.'

Then in with him to the pub. The little girl had tears in her eyes. I was sorry for her – that's the sort I am, very soft-hearted.

'All right,' I said. 'I'll go in and try to get my da out.'

But when I went in I saw it was no good. Her father was sitting on the windowsill, and behind him the blue bay and the white yachts showed like a newspaper photo through the mesh of the window screen. Father was walking up and down, his head bent, like a caged tiger.

'Capwell?' I heard him say in a low voice.

'Capwell I said,' replied the sailor.

'Evergreen?' said Father.

'Evergreen,' nodded the sailor.

'The oldest stock in Cork, you said?' whispered Father.

'Fifteenth century,' said the sailor.

Father looked at him with a gathering smile as though he thought it was all one of the sailor's jokes. Then he shook his head good-humouredly, and walked to the other side of the bar as though to say it was too much for him. Madness had out-ranged itself.

'The north side of the city,' said the sailor, growing heated at such disbelief, 'what is it only foreigners? People that came in from beyond the lamps a generation ago. Tramps and fiddlers and pipers.'

'They had the intellect,' Father said quietly.

'Intellect?' exclaimed the sailor. 'The north side?'

' 'Twas always given up to them,' said Father firmly.

'That's the first I heard of it,' said the sailor.

Father began to scribble with a couple of fingers on the palm of his left hand.

'Now,' he said gravely, 'I'll give you fair odds. I'll go back a hundred years with you. Tell me the name of a single out-standing man – now I said an *outstanding* man, mind you – that was born on the south side of the city in that time.'

'Daddy,' I said, pulling him by the coat-tails, 'you promised to take me up the cliffs.'

'In two minutes now,' he replied with a brief laugh, and, almost by second nature, handed me another penny.

That was four I had. J. J., a thoughtful poor soul, followed me out with two bottles of lemonade and a couple of packets of biscuits. The little girl and I ate and drank, sitting on the low wall outside the pub. Then we went down to the water's edge and tried to sail the boat, but, whatever was wrong with it, it would only float on its side; its sails got wringing wet, and we left them to dry while we listened to the organ of the merry-go-rounds from the other side of the bay.

It wasn't until late afternoon that the sailor and Father came out, and by this time there seemed to be no more than the breath of life between them. It was astonishing to me how friendly they were. Father had the sailor by the lapel of the jacket and was begging him to wait for the boat, but the sailor explained that he had given his solemn word to his wife to have the little girl home in time for bed and insisted that he'd have to go by the train. After he had departed, my father threw a long, lingering look at the sky, and seeing it was so late, slipped me another penny and retired to the bar till the siren went for the boat. They were hauling up the gangway when J. J. got him down.

It was late when we landed, and the full moon was riding over the river; a lovely, nippy September night; but I was tired and hungry and blown up with wind. We went up the hill in the moonlight and every few yards Father stopped to lay down the law. By this time he was ready to argue with anyone about anything. We came to the cathedral, and there were three old women sitting on the steps gossiping, their black shawls trailing like shadows on the pavement. It made me sick for home, a cup of hot cocoa, and my own warm bed.

Then suddenly under a gas lamp at the street-corner I saw a small figure in white. It was like an apparition. I was struck with terror and despair. I don't know if J. J. saw the same thing, but all at once he began to direct Father's attention to the cathedral and away from the figure in white.

'That's a beautiful tower,' he said in a husky voice.

Father stopped and screwed up his eyes to study it.

'What's beautiful about it?' he asked. 'I don't see anything very remarkable about that.'

'Ah, 'tis, man,' said J. J. reverently. 'That's a great tower.'

'Now, I'm not much in favour of towers,' said Father, tossing his head cantankerously. 'I don't see what use are towers. I'd sooner a nice plain limestone front with pillars like the Sand Quay.'

At the time I wasn't very concerned about the merits of Gothic and Renaissance, so I tried to help J. J. by tugging Father's hand. It was no good. One glance round and his eye took in the white figure at the other side of the road. He chuckled ominously and put his hand over his eyes, like a sailor on deck.

'Hard aport, mate!' he said. 'What do I see on my starboard bow?'

'Ah, nothing,' said J. J.

'Nothing?' echoed Father joyously. 'What sort of lookout man are you? ... Ahoy, shipmate!' he bawled across the road. 'Didn't your old skipper go home yet?'

'He did not,' cried the little girl – it was she of course – 'and let you leave him alone!'

'The thundering ruffian!' said my father in delight, and away he went across the road. 'What do he mean? A sailorman from the south side, drinking in my diocese! I'll have him ejected.'

'Daddy,' I wailed, with my heart in my boots. 'Come home, can't you?'

'Two minutes,' he said with a chuckle, and handed me another copper, the sixth.

The little girl was frantic. She scrawled and beat him about the legs with her fist, but he only laughed at her, and when the door opened he forced his way in with a shout: 'Anyone here from Valparaiso?'

J. J. sucked in his cheeks till he looked like a skeleton in the moonlight, and then nodded sadly and followed Father in. The door was bolted behind them and the little girl and I were left together on the pavement. The three old women on the cathedral steps got up and shuffled off down a cobbled laneway. The pair of us sat on the kerb and snivelled.

'What bad luck was on me this morning to meet you?' said the little girl.

' 'Twas on me the bad luck was,' I said, 'and your old fellow keeping my old fellow out.'

'Your old fellow is only a common labouring man,' said the little girl contemptuously, 'and my daddy says he's ignorant and conceited.'

'And your old fellow is only a sailor,' I retorted indignantly, 'and my father says all sailors are liars.'

'How dare you!' she said. 'My daddy is not a liar, and I hope he keeps your fellow inside all night, just to piece you out for your impudence.'

'I don't care,' I said with mock bravado. 'I can go home when I like and you can't – bah!'

'You'll have to wait till your father comes out.'

'I needn't. I can go home myself.'

'I dare you! You and your sailor suit!'

I could have let it pass but for her gibe at my suit; but that insult had to be avenged. I got up and took a few steps, just to show her. I thought she'd be afraid to stay behind alone, but she wasn't. She was too bitter. Of course, I had no intention of going home by myself at that hour of night. I stopped.

'Coward!' she said venomously. 'You're afraid.'

'I'll show you whether I'm afraid or not,' I said sulkily, and went off down Shandon Street – I who had never before been out alone after dark. I was terrified. It's no use swanking about it. I was simply terrified. I stopped every few yards, hoping she'd call out or that Father would come running after me. Neither happened, and at each dark laneway I shut my eyes. There was no sound but feet climbing this flight of steps or descending that. When I reached the foot of Shandon Street by the old graveyard, and saw the long, dark, winding hill before me, my courage gave out. I was afraid to go on and afraid to turn back.

Then I saw a friendly sign; a little huxter shop with a long flight of steps to the door, flanked by iron railings. High over the basement I could see the narrow window decorated in crinkly red paper, with sweet bottles and a few toys on view. Then I saw one toy that raised my courage. I counted my coppers again. There were six. I climbed the steps, went in the dark hallway, and turned right into the front room, which was used as the shop. A little old Mother Hubbard of a woman came out, rubbing her hands in her apron.

'Well, little boy?' she asked briskly.

'I want a dog, ma'am.'

'Sixpence apiece the dogs,' she said doubtfully. 'Have you sixpence?'

'I have, ma'am,' said I, and I counted out my coppers. She gave me the dog, a black, woolly dog with two beads for ears. I ran down the steps and up the road with my head high, whistling. I only wished that the little girl could see me now; she wouldn't say I was a coward. To show my contempt for the terrors of night I stood at the mouth of each laneway and looked down. I stroked the dog's fur, and when some shadow loomed up more frightening than the others I turned his head at it.

'Ssss!' I said. 'At him, boy! At him!'

When Mother opened the door I caught him and held him back.

'Down, Towser, down!' I said commandingly. 'It's only Mummy.'

My Da

It's funny the influence fathers can have on fellows – I mean without even realizing it. There was a lad called Stevie Leary living next door to us in Blarney Street. His mother and father had separated when he was only a baby, and his father had gone off to America and never been heard of after. His mother had left Stevie behind and followed him there, but of course she had never found him.

Stevie was a real comical artist. We all laughed at him but he didn't seem to mind. My mother had great pity for him because she thought he was a bit touched. She said he was a good poor slob. Even his own mother hadn't much to say for him. 'Ah, he'll never be the man his father was, ma'am,' she'd say mournfully, over-right the kid himself. He didn't seem to worry about that, either. He was a big overgrown streel of a boy with a fat round idiotic face and a rosy complexion, a walk that was more of a slide, and a shrill scolding old-woman's voice. He wore baggy knickerbockers and a man's cap several sizes too big for him.

Stevie took life with deadly seriousness. It might have been that his mother had told him the life story of some American millionaire, for he was full of enterprise, always in a hurry, and whenever he stopped it was as though someone were pulling the reins and forcing him to a halt. He slithered and skidded till he stopped, with his big moony face over one shoulder, like some good-natured old horse. He collected swill for the Mahonys who kept pigs, and delivered messages for the Delurys of the pub where his mother worked, and for a penny would undertake anything from minding the baby to buying the week's groceries. He had no false pride. He had a little tup-penny notebook he wrote his commissions in with a bit of puce pencil that he wet with his tongue, trying to look as much like a commercial traveller as he could, and with that queer crabbed air of his he'd rattle away in his shrill voice about what was the cheapest sort of meat to make soup of. 'You ought to try Reillys, ma'am. Reillys keeps grand stewing-beef.' He suggested modestly to Reillys that they might consider giving him a commission, but they wouldn't. He pretended to think we made fun of him only because we were jealous, because we were only kids and didn't know any better. He said no one need be poor! Look at him with a Post Office account; good money accumulating at two per cent! 'Aha, boy,' he said gloatingly, 'that's the way to get on!' The fellow really behaved as though the rest of us were halfwits. You couldn't help feeling he was touched.

There was only one obstacle to Stevie's progress towards a million, and that was his mother, a grand bosomy capacious woman whom my mother was very fond of. Sometimes they'd sit for a whole evening over the fire, taking snuff and connoisseuring about Mrs Leary's unfortunate marriage. Innocence and experience were nothing to them, with Mrs Leary saying in her husky voice that a man would never love you till he'd beat you, and that if it was the last breath in her body she'd have to hit back. 'That's how I lost my good looks, girl,' she would say. 'I had great feelings, and nothing ages a woman like the feelings.'

But she still had plenty of feelings left, and sometimes they got the upper hand of her. Stevie would be sitting outside the cottage of an evening, watching the kids playing with a smile that was both lonesome and superior, as befitted a fellow with a Post Office account, when some little girl would come up the road, bawling out the news.

'Stevie Leary, your old one is on it again.'

Stevie's smile would fade, and he would wander off aimlessly down the road, till, getting out of our sight, he put on his businessman's air, and darted briskly into each pub he passed in search of his mother.

'You didn't see my ma today, Miss O.?' he would shout. 'She's on it again.'

Eventually he would run her to earth in some snug with a

couple of cronies. Mrs Leary was never the lonesome sort of boozer; she liked admirers.

'God help us!' one of the hangers-on would say hypocritically when Stevie tried to detach them from their quarry, 'isn't he a lovely little boy, God bless him?'

'Ah, he'll never be the man his father was, ma'am,' Mrs Leary would say with resignation, taking another pinch of snuff.

'But with the help of God he'll be steadier,' another crony would add meaningly.

'Ah, what steady?' Mrs Leary would retort contemptuously. 'I wouldn't give a snap of my fingers for a man that wouldn't have a bit of the devil in him. Old mollies!'

It might be nightfall before Stevie manoeuvred her home, a mountain of a woman who'd have stunned him if she fell on him.

'Wisha, indeed and indeed, Mrs Leary,' Mother would say as she tried to settle her, 'you ought to be ashamed of yourself. Look at the cut of you!'

But before bedtime Mrs Leary would be on the prowl again, with Stevie crying: 'Ah, stop in, Ma, and I'll get it for you,' and his mother shouting: 'Gimme the money, can't you? Gimme the money, I say!'

With the low cunning of the drunkard she knew to a penny how much poor Stevie had, and night after night she shambled down to Miss O.'s with nothing showing under the peak of her shawl but one bleak, bloodshot eye; and tuppence by tuppence Stevie's savings vanished till he started life again with all the bounce gone out of him, as poor as any of us who had never heard the life story of an American millionaire. He tried to get her to regard it as a loan and pay him interest on it at the rate of a penny in the shilling, but a woman of such feelings couldn't be expected to understand the petty notions of finance. To be a proper millionaire you need a settled home life.

Then one night to everyone's astonishment Frankie Leary came home from America. There was nothing you could actually call a homecoming about it. Father and I were at the door when we spotted the strange man coming up the road; a lean,

leathery man with a long face, cold eyes, and a hard chin.
wouldn't have been surprised if you heard he came from the
North Pole. He went next door, and Father at once turned in
to the kitchen to ask Mother who he could be. There were
screams and sobs from next door. ' 'Tis never Frankie!' said
Mother, growing pale. 'But the man hadn't as much as a kit-
bag,' said Father. Ten minutes later Mrs Leary herself came in
to tell us. She was delirious with excitement. 'The old devil!'
she said with her eyes shining. 'I wouldn't doubt him. He never
lost it.' It seems that when she tried to embrace him in a wifely
way he merely said coldly that he had a crow to pluck with her,
and that when Stevie, who was equal to any social occasion,
asked him if he had had a nice journey, he never replied at all.
Of course, as Mother said, he might have had a nasty crossing.

For weeks Frankie's arrival kept Stevie in a state bordering
on hysteria. In one way Frankie was a disappointment, the first
American Stevie had heard of who returned home without a
rex. But that was only a trifle beside the real thing. For the
first time in his life Stevie had a father of his own like the rest
of us, and if he had given birth to him himself he couldn't have
had more old swank about it. America was an additional feather
in his cap; day in, day out, we heard nothing but the wonders
of America, houses and trains, taller and longer. No normal
son would ever have behaved like that, but then Stevie wasn't
normal. As fathers were generally called in for the sole purpose
of flaking hell out of us, Stevie felt it was up to him to go in
fear and trembling too; it gave him a sort of delighted satisfaction to refuse good money for going on a message, all because
of what his father might say. He turned down the money for
the pleasure of calling attention to the fact that he had a father;
pure showing off.

Frankie knew as little about being a father as Stevie did
about being a son, and compromised on an amateurish imitation of an elder brother. He soon discovered Stevie's passion
for America, and talked about it to him in a heavy, informative
way, while Stevie, in an appalling imitation of a public-house
expert, sat back with his hands in his trouser pockets. When
Frankie did check him it was about things like that, and the

effect on Stevie was magical. It was as though these were the
words of wisdom he'd been waiting for all his life. He began
deliberately trying to moderate his shuffle so that he wouldn't
have to pull himself up on the rein, and to break his voice of its
squeak. Stevie trying to be tough like his old fellow was one
of his funniest phases for, undoubtedly, Frankie was the man
he'd never be.

Frankie was a queer man, an arid, unnatural man. The first
evening my father and he talked at the door, Father described
him as 'a most superior, well-informed, manly chap', but he
changed his views the very next day when Frankie all but cut
him at the foot of Blarney Street. Father was a sociable creature; he felt he might have said something wrong; he begged
Mother to ask Mrs Leary if Frankie hadn't misunderstood
some remark of his, but Mrs Leary only laughed and said: 'He
never lost it.' 'I wouldn't doubt him,' and 'he never lost it,' two
highly ambiguous sayings, were as close as she ever got to
defining her husband's character. After that, Father put him
down as 'moody and contrary' and kept his distance.

But he had good points. He was steady; he didn't drink or
smoke. He made Mrs Leary give up the daily work and wear a
hat and coat instead of the shawl; he made Stevie give up the
swill and messages and learn to read and write, accomplish-
ments which were apparently omitted from the curriculum of
whatever millionaire Stevie was modelling himself on. The
change in the cottage was remarkable.

At times of course there were rows when Mrs Leary came
home with the sign of drink on her, but they weren't rows as
we understood them. Frankie didn't make smithereens of the
furniture or fling his wife and child out of doors in their night-
clothes the way other fathers did, but, trifling as they were,
they left Stevie shattered. He burst into tears and begged his
parents to agree.

One night about six months later Mrs Leary rambled in, a
bit more expansive than usual. She wasn't drunk, just amiable.
Frankie, who had been waiting for his tea, looked up from the
paper he was reading.

'What kept you?' he asked in his shrill voice.

'I ran into Lizzie Desmond at the Cross and we started talking,' said Mrs Leary, so snug in her hammock of whiskey that she never noticed the vessel begin to roll.

'Ye started drinking, I suppose,' said Frankie.

'Wisha, we had a couple of small ones,' said Mrs Leary. 'That old Cross is the windiest hole to stand talking in! Have you the kettle boiling, Stevie, boy?'

'You'd better remember what the small ones did for you before,' Frankie said grimly.

'And wasn't I well able for it?' she retorted, beginning to raise her voice.

'Whisht, Ma, whisht!' Stevie cried in an agony of fear. 'You know my da is only speaking for your good.'

'Speaking for my good?' she trumpeted, her feelings overcoming her all at once at the suggestion that she needed such correction. 'How dare you!' she added to Frankie, drawing herself up with great dignity and letting the small ones speak for her. 'Is that my thanks after all I done for you, crossing the briny ocean after you, you insignificant little gnat?'

'What's that you said?' asked Frankie, throwing down his paper and striding up to her with his fists clenched.

'Gnat!' she repeated scornfully, looking him up and down. 'If I might have married a man itself instead of an insignificant little article like you that wouldn't make a bolt for a back door!'

Even before Stevie knew what he was up to, Frankie drew back his fist and gave it to her full in the mouth. Mrs Leary let one great shriek out of her and fell. Stevie, who was as strange as my mother to the ways of a man in love, let out another shriek and threw himself on his knees beside her.

'Oh, Ma, look at me, look at me!' he bawled distractedly. 'I'm Stevie, your own little boy.'

That didn't produce whatever it was intended to produce in the way of response, so Stevie cocked an eye up at his father.

'Will I get the priest for her, Dadda?' he asked in languishing tones. 'I think she's dying.'

'Get to hell out of this,' said Frankie shortly. 'It's time you were in bed.'

It wasn't, but Stevie knew better than to contradict him. A little later Frankie went to bed himself, leaving his wife lying on the floor – dead, no doubt. Mother wanted to go in to her, but Father stopped that at once.

'Now,' he said oracularly, 'there's a man in the house,' and for years afterwards I found myself at intervals trying to analyse the finality of that pronouncement. An hour later, Mrs Leary got up and made herself a cup of tea. 'She can't be so badly hurt,' said my mother with relief. I could see she was full of pity for Stevie, having to allow his mother to remain so long like that, without assistance. There was a man in the house all right.

Next morning, the poor kid woke with all the troubles of the world on him. He poured them all out to Mother. Things were desperate in the home. All the light he had on it was one sermon he had heard at a men's retreat which he shouldn't have attended, in which the missioner had said that a child was the great bond between the parents. 'Would you say I'd be a bond, Mrs O.?' squeaked Stevie. Doing his best to be a bond, he gave his mother a pot of tea in bed and made his father's breakfast. After Frankie had gone to work, he begged his mother to stay in bed, and even offered to bring her up the porter, but she wouldn't. Her pride was too hurt. Stevie knew she was much more frightened of Frankie than he was, but her pride wouldn't let her yield.

In the afternoon he found her again in a pub in town and brought her home, shaking his head and cluck-clucking fondly over her. She was a sight, the hood of her shawl pulled down over her face, and a bloodshot eye and a bruised mouth just visible beneath it. Stevie did all he could to make her presentable; brewed her tea, washed her face, combed her hair, and even tried to make her take shelter with us and leave him to deal with his father, but compromise was an expression she didn't understand.

At six Frankie came in like a thundercloud, and Stevie bustled round him eagerly and clumsily, getting his supper.

He had everything neat and shining. In his capacity as bond he had reverted to type.

'You'd like a couple of buttered eggs?' he squeaked cheerfully. 'You would to be sure. Dwyers keeps grand eggs.'

Neither of his parents addressed one another. After supper Frankie took his cap to go out.

'You won't be late, Dadda?' Stevie asked anxiously, but his father didn't reply. Stevie went to the door after him and watched him down the road.

'I'd be afraid he mightn't come back,' he said.

'That he mightn't!' his mother said piously. 'We done without him before and we can do without him again. Conceited jackeen!'

Then he came into our house to report his lack of success as a bond. What made it so queer was that he sounded cheerful.

'A father is a great loss, Mr O.' he said to my father. 'A house is never the same without a man.'

'You ought to see is he in your Uncle John's,' said my mother a bit anxiously.

'I wouldn't say so,' said Stevie. 'The sort my da is, he'd be too proud. He wouldn't give it to say to them.'

The child showed real insight. However he'd managed it, Frankie was off on his travels again, with a fresh disillusionment to fly from. Even my mother didn't blame him, though she thought he should have done something for Stevie. Little by little, the old air of fecklessness and neglect came back. Stevie was completely wretched – a fellow who couldn't mind a father when he got one. He lost his bounce entirely, and took to mooning about the chapel, lighting candles for his father's return. Mrs Leary went back to the shawl and the daily work, Stevie to the swill and the messages, all exactly as though Frankie had never returned, as though it had all been a dream.

But if it had become a dream, the dream had the power of robbing reality of its innocence. Because it was the only thing Frankie had asked of him, the only way in which he could get closer to his father, Stevie took to attending night school and joined the public library. Sometimes I met him coming back over the New Bridge with his books and we exchanged impressions. Clearly he didn't think much of the Wild West stories I loved.

Stevie being intellectual made us laugh, but it was nothing to what followed, because, as a result of something the teacher in the Technical School said to the Canon, the Canon saw Stevie, and Mrs Leary got regular cleaning-work in the presbytery while Stevie went to the seminary. It seemed he had suddenly discovered a vocation for the priesthood!

This was no laughing matter. It was almost a scandal. Of course, even if he got ordained, it wouldn't be the same thing as Mrs Delury's son who had been to Maynooth; it could only mean the Foreign Mission, but you'd think that even the Foreign Mission would draw a line. Mother, in spite of her pity for him, was shocked. I was causing her concern enough as it was, for I had just lost my faith for the first time, and, though she never put it in so many words, I fancy she felt that if the Church had to fall back on people like Stevie Leary, I might have some reason.

I remember the first time I saw him in his clerical black I realized that he had heard about my losing my faith, for he behaved as though I had lost the week's wages. It was exactly like our meetings on the way to the library. I could almost hear him say that no one need lose his faith in the same tone in which, as a kid, he used to say that no one need be poor. All you had to do was put it in the Post Office. 'Aha, boy, that's the way to get on!' I felt that he might at least have shown some sympathy for me.

Not that anyone showed him much – except Mother. When he said his first Mass in the parish church we all turned up. Mrs Delury, her two sons and a daughter, were all there, boiling with rage to think of their charwoman's son being a priest like their own Miah, and blaming it all on America. Such a country!

Stevie preached on the Good Shepherd and, whether it was the excitement or the sight of four Delurys in one pew – a sight to daunt the boldest – he got all mixed up between the ninety-nine and the one; though in his maundering, enthusiastic style it didn't make much difference. But you could almost hear the Delurys crowing.

My mother and I went round to the sacristy to get his blessing (by this time I had got back my faith and didn't lose it again for another two years), but as we knelt I could scarcely keep my face straight because, God forgive me, I expected at every moment that Stevie would say: 'Wouldn't a few pounds of stewing-beef be better, ma'am?'

The Opposition, headed by Mrs Delury, was in session outside the church when we left.

'Poor Father Stephen got a bit mixed in his sums,' Mrs Delury said regretfully.

'Ah, the dear knows, wouldn't anybody?' retorted my mother, flushed and angry.

'I don't suppose in America they'll notice much difference,' said Mrs Delury.

'America?' I said. 'Is that where he's going?'

And suddenly it struck me with the force of a revelation that fathers had their good points after all. That evening I dropped in on the Learys. I wanted to see Stevie again. I had realized after Mass that, like the Delurys, I had for years been living with a shadow-Stevie, a comic kid who had disappeared ages ago under our eyes without our noticing. I wasn't surprised to meet for the first time an unusually intelligent and sensitive young man.

'Ah, he'll love it in America, Larry,' his mother said in her snug, husky voice. ''Twill be new life to him; fine openhanded people instead of the articles we have around here that think they're somebody. The dear knows, I wouldn't mind going back myself.'

But we all knew there wasn't much chance of that. If there's one thing a young priest has to deny himself, it's a mother whose feelings become too much for her, and though the whole time he was at home she was irreproachable, the night she saw him off, a good-natured policeman had to bring her home and my mother put her to bed.

'Ah, indeed and indeed, Mrs Leary,' said my mother quivering with indignation to see a woman so degrade herself, 'you ought to be ashamed of yourself. What would Father Stephen say if he saw you now?'

But there was no Father Stephen to see her, then or any other time. Stevie had at last become a man his father was and left us all far behind him.

News for the Church

When Father Cassidy drew back the shutter of the confessional he was a little surprised at the appearance of the girl at the other side of the grille. It was dark in the box but he could see she was young, of medium height and build, with a face that was full of animation and charm. What struck him most was the long pale slightly freckled cheeks, pinned high up behind the grey-blue eyes, giving them a curiously oriental slant.

She wasn't a girl from the town, for he knew most of these by sight and many of them by something more, being notoriously an easygoing confessor. The other priests said that one of these days he'd give up hearing confessions altogether on the ground that there was no such thing as sin and that even if there was it didn't matter. This was part and parcel of his exceedingly angular character, for though he was kind enough to individual sinners, his mind was full of obscure abstract hatreds. He hated England; he hated the Irish Government, and he particularly hated the middle classes, though so far as anyone knew none of them had ever done him the least bit of harm. He was a heavy-built man, slow-moving and slow-thinking with no neck and a Punchinello chin, a sour wine-coloured face, pouting crimson lips, and small blue hot-tempered eyes.

'Well, my child,' he grunted in a slow and mournful voice that sounded for all the world as if he had pebbles in his mouth, 'how long is it since your last confession?'

'A week, Father,' she replied in a clear firm voice. It surprised him a little, for though she didn't look like one of the tough shots, neither did she look like the sort of girl who goes to confession every week. But with women you could never tell. They were all contrary, saints and sinners.

'And what sins did you commit since then?' he asked encouragingly.

'I told lies, Father.'

'Anything else?'

'I used bad language, Father.'

'I'm surprised at you,' he said with mock seriousness. 'An educated girl with the whole of the English language at your disposal! What sort of bad language?'

'I used the Holy Name, Father.'

'Ach,' he said with a frown, 'you ought to know better than that. There's no great harm in damning and blasting but blasphemy is a different thing. To tell you the truth,' he added, being a man of great natural honesty, 'there isn't much harm in using the Holy Name either. Most of the time there's no intentional blasphemy but at the same time it coarsens the character. It's all the little temptations we don't indulge in that give us true refinement. Anything else?'

'I was tight, Father.'

'Hm,' he grunted. This was rather more the sort of girl he had imagined her to be; plenty of devilment but no real badness. He liked her bold and candid manner. There was no hedging or false modesty about her as about most of his women penitents. 'When you say you were "tight" do you mean you were just merry or what?'

'Well, I mean I passed out,' she replied candidly with a shrug.

'I don't call that "tight", you know,' he said sternly. 'I call that beastly drunk. Are you often tight?'

'I'm a teacher in a convent school so I don't get much chance,' she replied ruefully.

'In a convent school?' he echoed with new interest. Convent schools and nuns were another of his phobias; he said they were turning the women of the country into imbeciles. 'Are you on holidays now?'

'Yes. I'm on my way home.'

'You don't live here then?'

'No, down the country.'

'And is it the convent that drives you to drink?' he asked with an air of unshakeable gravity.

'Well,' she replied archly, 'you know what nuns are.'

'I do,' he agreed in a mournful voice while he smiled at her through the grille. 'Do you drink with your parents' knowledge?' he added anxiously.

'Oh, yes. Mummy is dead but Daddy doesn't mind. He lets us take a drink with him.'

'Does he do that on principle or because he's afraid of you?' the priest asked dryly.

'Ah, I suppose a little of both,' she answered gaily, responding to his queer dry humour. It wasn't often that women did, and he began to like this one a lot.

'Is your mother long dead?' he asked sympathetically.

'Seven years,' she replied, and he realized that she couldn't have been much more than a child at the time and had grown up without a mother's advice and care. Having worshipped his own mother, he was always sorry for people like that.

'Mind you,' he said paternally, his hands joined on his fat belly, 'I don't want you to think there's any harm in a drop of drink. I take it myself. But I wouldn't make a habit of it if I were you. You see, it's all very well for old jossers like me that have the worst of their temptations behind them, but yours are all ahead and drink is a thing that grows on you. You need never be afraid of going wrong if you remember that your mother may be watching you from heaven.'

'Thanks, Father,' she said, and he saw at once that his gruff appeal had touched some deep and genuine spring of feeling in her. 'I'll cut it out altogether.'

'You know, I think I would,' he said gravely, letting his eyes rest on her for a moment. 'You're an intelligent girl. You can get all the excitement you want out of life without that. What else?'

'I had bad thoughts, Father.'

'Ach,' he said regretfully, 'we all have them. Did you indulge them?'

'Yes, Father.'

'Have you a boy?'

'Not a regular: just a couple of fellows hanging round.'

'Ah, that's worse than none at all,' he said crossly. 'You ought to have a boy of your own. I know there's old cranks that will tell you different, but sure, that's plain foolishness. Those things are only fancies, and the best cure for them is something real. Anything else?'

There was a moment's hesitation before she replied but it was enough to prepare him for what was coming.

'I had carnal intercourse with a man, Father,' she said quietly and deliberately.

'You what?' he cried, turning on her incredulously. 'You had carnal intercourse with a man? At your age?'

'I know,' she said with a look of distress. 'It's awful.'

'It is awful,' he replied slowly and solemnly. 'And how often did it take place?'

'Once, Father – I mean twice, but on the same occasion.'

'Was it a married man?' he asked, frowning.

'No, Father, single. At least I think he was single,' she added with sudden doubt.

'You had carnal intercourse with a man,' he said accusingly, 'and you don't know if he was married or single!'

'I assumed he was single,' she said with real distress. 'He was the last time I met him but, of course, that was five years ago.'

'Five years ago? But you must have been only a child then.'

'That's all, of course,' she admitted. 'He was courting my sister, Kate, but she wouldn't have him. She was running round with her present husband at the time and she only kept him on a string for amusement. I knew that and I hated her because he was always so nice to me. He was the only one that came to the house who treated me like a grown-up. But I was only fourteen, and I suppose he thought I was too young for him.'

'And were you?' Father Cassidy asked ironically. For some reason he had the idea that this young lady had no proper idea of the enormity of her sin and he didn't like it.

'I suppose so,' she replied modestly. 'But I used to feel awful, being sent up to bed and leaving him downstairs with Kate when I knew she didn't care for him. And then when I met him again the whole thing came back. I sort of went all soft inside. It's never the same with another fellow as it is with the first fellow you fall for. It's exactly as if he had some sort of hold over you.'

'If you were fourteen at the time,' said Father Cassidy, setting aside the obvious invitation to discuss the power of first love, 'you're only nineteen now.'

'That's all.'

'And do you know,' he went on broodingly, 'that unless you can break yourself of this terrible vice once for all it'll go on like that till you're fifty?'

'I suppose so,' she said doubtfully, but he saw that she didn't suppose anything of the kind.

'You suppose so!' he snorted angrily. 'I'm telling you so. And what's more,' he went on, speaking with all the earnestness at his command, 'it won't be just one man but dozens of men, and it won't be decent men but whatever low-class pups you can find who'll take advantage of you – the same horrible, mortal sin, week in week out till you're an old woman.'

'Ah, still, I don't know,' she said eagerly, hunching her shoulders ingratiatingly, 'I think people do it as much from curiosity as anything else.'

'Curiosity?' he repeated in bewilderment.

'Ah, you know what I mean,' she said with a touch of impatience. 'People make such a mystery of it!'

'And what do you think they should do?' he asked ironically. 'Publish it in the papers?'

'Well, God knows, 'twould be better than the way some of them go on,' she said in a rush. 'Take my sister Kate, for instance. I admit she's a couple of years older than me and she brought me up and all the rest of it, but in spite of that we were always good friends. She showed me her love letters and I showed her mine. I mean, we discussed things as equals, but ever since that girl got married you'd hardly recognize her. She talks to no one only other married women, and they get in a huddle in a corner and whisper, whisper, whisper, and the moment you come into the room they begin to talk about the weather, exactly as if you were a blooming kid! I mean you can't help feeling 'tis something extraordinary.'

'Don't you try and tell me anything about immorality,' said

Father Cassidy angrily. 'I know all about it already. It may begin as curiosity but it ends as debauchery. There's no vice you could think of that gets a grip on you quicker and degrades you worse, and don't you make any mistake about it, young woman! Did this man say anything about marrying you?'

'I don't think so,' she replied thoughtfully, 'but of course that doesn't mean anything. He's an airy, light-hearted sort of fellow and it mightn't occur to him.'

'I never supposed it would,' said Father Cassidy grimly. 'Is he in a position to marry?'

'I suppose he must be since he wanted to marry Kate,' she replied with fading interest.

'And is your father the sort of man that can be trusted to talk to him?'

'Daddy?' she exclaimed aghast. 'But I don't want Daddy brought into it.'

'What you want, young woman,' said Father Cassidy with sudden exasperation, 'is beside the point. Are you prepared to talk to this man yourself?'

'I suppose so,' she said with a wondering smile. 'But about what?'

'About what?' repeated the priest angrily. 'About the little matter he so conveniently overlooked, of course.'

'You mean ask him to marry me?' she cried incredulously. 'But I don't want to marry him.'

Father Cassidy paused for a moment and looked at her anxiously through the grille. It was growing dark inside the church, and for one horrible moment he had the feeling that somebody was playing an elaborate and most tasteless joke on him.

'Do you mind telling me,' he inquired politely, 'am I mad or are you?'

'But I mean it, Father,' she said eagerly. 'It's all over and done with now. It's something I used to dream about, and it was grand, but you can't do a thing like that a second time.'

'You can't what?' he asked sternly.

'I mean, I suppose you can, really,' she said, waving her piously joined hands at him as if she were handcuffed, 'but you can't get back the magic of it. Terry is light-hearted and good-natured, but I couldn't live with him. He's completely irresponsible.'

'And what do you think you are?' cried Father Cassidy, at the end of his patience. 'Have you thought of all the dangers you're running, girl? If you have a child who'll give you work? If you have to leave this country to earn a living what's going to become of you? I tell you it's your bounden duty to marry this man if he can be got to marry you – which, let me tell you,' he added with a toss of his great head, 'I very much doubt.'

'To tell you the truth I doubt it myself,' she replied with a shrug that fully expressed her feelings about Terry and nearly drove Father Cassidy insane. He looked at her for a moment or two and then an incredible idea began to dawn on his bothered old brain. He sighed and covered his face with his hand.

'Tell me,' he asked in a far-away voice, 'when did this take place?'

'Last night, Father,' she said gently, almost as if she were glad to see him come to his senses again.

'My God,' he thought despairingly, 'I was right!'

'In town, was it?' he went on.

'Yes, Father. We met on the train coming down.'

'And where is he now?'

'He went home this morning, Father.'

'Why didn't you do the same?'

'I don't know, Father,' she replied doubtfully as though the question had now only struck herself for the first time.

'Why didn't you go home this morning?' he repeated angrily. 'What were you doing round town all day?'

'I suppose I was walking,' she replied uncertainly.

'And of course you didn't tell anyone?'

'I hadn't anyone to tell,' she said plaintively. 'Anyway,' she added with a shrug, 'it's not the sort of thing you can tell people.'

'No, of course,' said Father Cassidy. 'Only a priest,' he added grimly to himself. He saw now how he had been taken in. This little trollop, wandering about town in a daze of bliss, had to tell someone her secret, and he, a good-natured old fool of sixty, had allowed her to use him as a confidant. A philosopher of sixty letting Eve, aged nineteen, tell him all about the apple! He could never live it down.

Then the fighting blood of the Cassidys began to warm in him. Oh, couldn't he, though? He had never tasted the apple himself, but he knew a few things about apples in general and that apple in particular that little Miss Eve wouldn't learn in a whole lifetime of apple-eating. Theory might have its drawbacks but there were times when it was better than practice. 'All right, my lass,' he thought grimly, 'we'll see which of us knows most!'

In a casual tone he began to ask her questions. They were rather intimate questions, such as a doctor or priest may ask, and, feeling broadminded and worldly-wise in her new experience, she answered courageously and straightforwardly, trying to suppress all signs of her embarrassment. It emerged only once or twice, in a brief pause before she replied. He stole a furtive look at her to see how she was taking it, and once more he couldn't withhold his admiration. But she couldn't keep it up. First she grew uncomfortable and then alarmed, frowning and shaking herself in her clothes as if something were biting her. He grew graver and more personal. She didn't see his purpose; she only saw that he was stripping off veil after veil of romance, leaving her with nothing but a cold, sordid, cynical adventure like a bit of greasy meat on a plate.

'And what did he do next?' he asked.

'Ah,' she said in disgust, 'I didn't notice.'

'You didn't notice!' he repeated ironically.

'But does it make any difference?' she burst out despairingly, trying to pull the few shreds of illusion she had left more tightly about her.

'I presume you thought so when you came to confess it,' he replied sternly.

'But you're making it sound so beastly!' she wailed.

'And wasn't it?' he whispered, bending closer, lips pursed and brows raised. He had her now, he knew.

'Ah, it wasn't, Father,' she said earnestly. 'Honest to God it wasn't. At least at the time I didn't think it was.'

'No,' he said grimly, 'you thought it was a nice little story to run and tell your sister. You won't be in such a hurry to tell her now. Say an Act of Contrition.'

She said it.

'And for your penance say three Our Fathers and three Hail Marys.'

He knew that was hitting below the belt, but he couldn't resist the parting shot of a penance such as he might have given a child. He knew it would rankle in that fanciful little head of hers when all his other warnings were forgotten. Then he drew the shutter and didn't open the farther one. There was a noisy woman behind, groaning in an excess of contrition. The mere volume of sound told him it was drink. He felt he needed a breath of fresh air.

He went down the aisle creakily on his heavy policeman's-feet and in the dusk walked up and down the path before the presbytery, head bowed, hands behind his back. He saw the girl come out and descend the steps under the massive fluted columns of the portico, a tiny, limp, dejected figure. As she reached the pavement she pulled herself together with a jaunty twitch of her shoulders and then collapsed again. The city lights went on and made globes of coloured light in the mist. As he returned to the church he suddenly began to chuckle, a fat good-natured chuckle, and as he passed the statue of St Anne, patron of marriageable girls, he almost found himself giving her a wink.

Freedom

When I was interned during the war with the British I dreamed endlessly of escape. As internment camps go, ours was pretty good. We had a theatre, games, and classes, and some of the classes were first-rate.

It was divided into two areas, North Camp and South, and the layout of the huts was sufficiently varied to give you a feeling of change when you went for a stroll round the wires. The tall wooden watchtowers, protected from the weather by canvas sheets, which commanded the barbed wire at intervals had a sort of ragged functional beauty of their own. You could do a five-mile walk there before breakfast and not feel bored.

But I ached to get away. It is almost impossible to describe how I ached. In the evenings I walked round the camp and always stopped at least once on a little hillock in the North Camp which had the best view of the flat green landscape of Kildare that stretched all round us for miles. It was brilliantly green, and the wide crowded skies had all the incredible atmospheric effects of flat country, with veil after veil of mist or rain even on the finest days, and I thought of the tinker families drifting or resting in the shadow of the hedges while summer lasted. God, I used to think, if only I could escape I'd never stop, summer or winter, but just go on and on, making my fire under a hedge and sleeping in a barn or under an upturned cart. Night and day I'd go on, maybe for years, maybe till I died. If only I could escape!

But there isn't any escape. I saw that even in the camp itself. I became friendly with two prisoners, Matt Deignan and Mick Stewart, both from Cork. They were nice lads; Mick sombre, reserved, and a bit lazy; Matt noisy, emotional, and energetic. They messed together and Matt came in for most of the work. That wasn't all he came in for. When Mick was in one of his

violent moods and had to have someone to wrestle with, Matt
was the victim. Mick wrestled with him, ground his arms behind his back, made him yelp with pain and plead for mercy.
Sometimes he reduced Matt to tears, and for hours Matt
wouldn't speak to him. It never went further than that though.
Matt was Caliban to Mick's Prospero and had to obey. He
would come to me, a graceless gawk with a moony face, and
moan to me about Mick's cruelty and insolence, but this was
only because he knew Mick liked me, and he hoped to squelch
Mick out of my mouth. If anyone else dared to say a word
against Mick he mocked at them. They were jealous!

Matt had a job in the Quartermaster's store, the Quartermaster, one Clancy, being some sort of eminent, distant cousin
of whom Matt was enormously proud. Mick and he both dossed
in J Hut in the North Camp. Now J was always a rather tony
hut, quite different from Q, where I hung out, which was
nothing but a municipal slaughterhouse. The tone of J was kept
up by about a dozen senior officers and politicians, businessmen and the like. The hut leader, Jim Brennan, a tough little
Dublin mason whom I admired, though not class himself, liked
class: he liked businessmen and fellows who wore silk pyjamas
and university students who could tell him all about God, VD,
and the next world. It broadened a man's mind a lot. These got
off lightly; either they had doctor's certificates to prove they
couldn't do fatigues or they had nominal jobs, which meant
they didn't have to do them. You couldn't blame Jim; it was
his hut, and he kept it like a battleship, and to get into it at all
was considered a bit of luck. Nor did the other men in the hut
object; they might be only poor country lads, but, like Jim,
they enjoyed mixing with fellows of a different class and listening to arguments about religion over the stove at night. It might
be the only opportunity most of them would ever have of hearing anything except about drains and diseases of cattle, and
they were storing it up. It was a thoroughly happy hut, and it
rather surprised me that two attempts at tunnelling had begun
from it; if it wasn't that the occupants wanted to show off their
intelligence, you wouldn't know what they wanted to escape for.

But Mick Stewart rather resented the undemocratic tone of

the hut and was careful to keep the camp aristocracy at a distance. When someone like Jack Costello, the draper, addressed Mick with what he thought undue familiarity, Mick pretended not to hear. Costello was surprised and Brennan was seriously displeased. He thought it disrespectful. He never noticed Mick except to give him an order. A couple of times he made him go over a job twice, partly to see it was properly done, partly to put Mick in his place.

Now, Mick was one of those blokes who never know they have a place. One day he just struck. While the others continued scrubbing he threw himself on his bed with his hands under his head and told the hut leader to do it himself. He did it with an icy calm which anyone who knew Mick would have known meant danger.

'You mean you call that clean?' Brennan asked, standing at the end of Mick's bed with his hands in his trouser pockets and his old cap over one eye.

'It's not a matter of opinion,' Mick said in his rather high-pitched, piping voice.

'Oh, isn't it?' asked Brennan and then called over Jack Costello. 'Jack,' he continued mildly, 'is that what you'd call clean?'

'Ah, come on, Stewart, come on!' Costello said in his best 'Arise, Ye Sons of Erin' manner. 'Don't be a blooming passenger!'

'I didn't know I asked your advice, Costello,' Mick said frostily, 'but as you seem to be looking for a job as a deckhand, fire ahead!'

'I certainly will,' Costello said gamely. 'Just to show I'm not too proud to be a deckhand.'

'No, you won't, Jack,' Brennan said heavily. 'There's going to be no passengers on this boat. Are you going to obey orders, Stewart?'

'If you mean am I going to do every job twice, I'm not,' replied Mick with a glare.

'Good enough,' Brennan said moodily as he turned away. 'We'll see about that.'

Now, I should perhaps have explained that the camp duplicated the whole British organization. Each morning we stood to attention at the foot of our beds to be counted, but one of our own officers always accompanied the counting party and ostensibly it was for him and not for the British officer that we paraded. It was the same with everything else; we recognized only our own officers. The Quartermaster drew the stores from the British and we received them from him and signed for them to him. The mail was sorted and delivered by our own post-office staff. We had our cooks, our doctors, our teachers and actors – even our police. Because, if one of our fellows was caught pinching another man's stuff, we had our own police to arrest him and our own military court to try him. In this way, we of the rank and file never came into contact at all with our jailers.

That morning two of the camp police, wearing tricolour armlets, came to march Mick down to the hut where his case was to be tried. One of them was a great galumphing lout called Kenefick, a bit of a simpleton, who cracked heavy jokes with Mick because he felt so self-conscious with his armlet. The case was heard in the camp office. When I passed I saw Matt Deignan outside, looking nervous and lonely. I stopped to talk with him and Brennan passed in, sulky and stubborn, without as much as a glance at either of us. Matt burst into a long invective against him, and I tried to shut him up, because in spite of his boorishness I respected Brennan.

'Ah, well,' I said, 'you can't put all the blame on Brennan. You know quite well that Mick is headstrong too.'

'Headstrong?' yelped Matt, ready to eat me. 'And wouldn't he want to be with a dirty lout like that?'

'Brennan is no lout,' I said. 'He's a fine soldier.'

'He is,' Matt said bitterly. 'He'd want to walk on you.'

'That's what soldiers are for,' I said, but Matt wasn't in a mood for facetiousness.

The court seemed to be a long time sitting, and it struck me that it might have been indiscreet enough to start an argument with Mick. This would have been a long operation. But at last he came out, a bit red but quite pleased with himself, and I decided that if there had been an argument he had got the better of it. We set off for a brisk walk round the camp. Mick would talk of everything except the case. Mick all out! He knew poor Matt was broken down with anxiety and was determined on toughening him.

'Well,' I said at last, 'what's the verdict?'

'Oh, that business!' he said contemptuously. 'Just what you'd expect.'

'And what's the sentence? Death or a five-year dip?'

'A week's fatigues.'

'That's not so bad,' I said.

'Not so bad?' cried Matt, almost in tears. 'And for what? Pure spite because Mick wouldn't kowtow to them. 'Tis all that fellow Costello, Mick boy,' he went on with a tragic air. 'I never liked him. He's the fellow that's poisoning them against you.'

'He's welcome,' Mick said frostily, deprecating all this vulgar emotionalism of Matt's. 'I'm not doing extra fatigues for them.'

'And you're right, Mick,' exclaimed Matt, halting. 'You're right. I'd see them in hell first.'

'You don't mean you're going to refuse to obey the staff?' I asked doubtfully.

'What else can I do?' Mick asked in a shrill complaining voice. 'Don't you realize what will happen if I let Brennan get away with this? He'll make my life a misery.'

'Starting a row with the camp command isn't going to make it exactly a honeymoon,' I said.

It didn't, but even I was astonished at the feeling roused by Mick's rebellion. Men who knew that he and I were friendly attacked him to me. No one said a word in his favour. And it wasn't that they were worried by the thing that worried me – that right or wrong, the camp command was the only elected authority in the camp – oh, no. Mick was disloyal to the cause, disloyal to the camp; worst of all, he was putting on airs. You would think that men who were rebels themselves and suffering for their views would have some sympathy for him.

'But the man is only sticking out for what he thinks are his rights,' I protested.

'Rights?' one man echoed wonderingly. 'What rights has he? Haven't we all to work?'

After a while I gave up arguing. It left me with the feeling that liberty wasn't quite such a clear-cut issue as I had believed it. Clancy, the Quartermaster, though himself one of the staff, was the most reasonable man on the other side. No doubt he felt he had to be because Mick was his cousin's friend. He was a gallant little man, small, fiery, and conscientious, and never really himself till he began to blaspheme. This wasn't yet a subject for blasphemy so he wasn't quite himself. He grasped me firmly by the shoulder, stared at me closely with his bright blue eyes and then looked away into an infinite distance.

'Jack,' he said in a low voice, 'between friends, tell that boy, Stewart, to have sense. The Commandant is very vexed. He's a severe man. I wouldn't like to be in Stewart's shoes if he crosses him again.'

'I suppose ye'd never use your brains and send Stewart and Matt to Q Hut?' I asked. 'It's only the way Mick and Brennan don't get on, and two human beings would improve Q Hut enormously.'

'Done!' he exclaimed, holding out his hand in a magnificent gesture. 'The minute he has his fatigues done, I'll tell the Commandant.'

I put that solution up to Mick and he turned it down in the most reasonable way in the world. That was one thing I was learning: your true rebel is nothing if not reasonable; it is only his premises that are dotty. Mick explained patiently that he couldn't agree to a compromise which would still leave him with a stain on his character because if ever we resurrected the army again and the army got down to keeping records it would count as a black mark against him.

'You mean for a pension?' I said, turning nasty, but Mick didn't realize that. He only thought it was rather crude of me to be so materialistic about a matter of principle. I was beginning to wonder if my own premises were quite sound.

Next morning I went over to J Hut to see how things were panning out. They looked pretty bad to me. It was a large, light, airy hut like a theatre with a low wooden partition down the middle and the beds ranged at either side of the partition and along the walls. It was unusually full for that hour of the morning, and there was a peculiar feeling you only get from a mob which is just on the point of getting out of hand. Mick was lying on his own bed, and Matt sitting on the edge of his, talking to him. No one seemed interested in them. The rest were sitting round the stove or fooling with macramé bags, waiting to see what happened. Three beds down from Mick was a handsome young Wexford fellow called Howard, also lying on his bed and ostensibly talking to his buddy. He saw me come in and raised his voice.

'The trouble is,' he was saying, 'people who won't pull their weight would be better at the other side of the wire.'

'Are you referring to me, Howard?' Mick asked harshly.

Howard sat up and turned a beaming adolescent face on him. 'As a matter of fact I am, Stewart,' he said.

'We were on the right side before ever ye were heard of, Howard,' bawled Matt. 'What the hell did ye ever do in Wexford beyond shooting a couple of misfortunate policemen?'

I started talking feverishly to avert the row, but fortunately just then Kenefick and another policeman of the right sort came in. This time they showed no embarrassment and there was nothing in the least matey about their attitude. It gave their tricolour armlets a certain significance. As we followed them out the whole hut began to hiss. Matt turned as though something had struck him but I pushed him out. It was all much worse than I expected.

Again Matt and I had to wait outside the office while the trial went on, but this time I wasn't feeling quite so light-hearted, and as for Matt, I could see it was the most tragic moment of his life. Never before had he thought of himself as a traitor, an enemy of society, but that was what they were trying to make of him.

This time when Mick emerged he had the two policemen with him. He tried to maintain a defiant air, but even he looked depressed.

'What happened, Mick?' bawled Matt, hurling himself on him like a distracted mother of nine.

'You're not supposed to talk to the prisoner,' said Kenefick.

'Ah, shut up you, Kenefick!' I snapped. 'What's the result, Mick?'

'Oh, I believe I'm going to jail,' said Mick, laughing without amusement.

'Going where?' I asked incredulously.

'So I'm told,' he replied with a shrug.

'But what jail?'

'Damned if I know,' he said, and suddenly began to laugh with genuine amusement.

'You'll know soon enough,' growled Kenefick, who seemed to resent the laughter as a slight on his office.

'Cripes, Kenefick,' I said, 'you missed your vocation.'

It really was extraordinary, how everything in that camp became a sort of crazy duplicate of something in the outside world. Nothing but an armlet had turned a good-natured halfwit like Kenefick into a real policeman, exactly like the ones who had terrified me as a kid when I'd been playing football on the road. I had noticed it before; how the post-office clerks became sulky and uncommunicative; how the fellows who played girls in the Sunday-evening shows made scenes and threw up their parts exactly like film stars, and some of the teachers started sending them notes. But now the whole crazy pattern seemed to be falling into place. At any moment I expected to find myself skulking away from Kenefick.

We moved in a group between the huts to the rather unpleasant corner of the camp behind the cookhouse. Then I suddenly saw what Kenefick meant. There was a little hut you wouldn't notice, a small storeroom which might have been a timekeeper's hut in a factory only that its one small window had bars. The pattern was complete at last; as well as store, school, theatre, church, post office, and police court we now had a real jail of our own. Inside it had bedboards, a three-biscuit mattress, and blankets. They had thought of everything down to the bucket. It amused me so much that I scarcely felt any emotion at saying goodbye to Mick. But Matt was beside himself with rage.

'Where are you off to?' I asked as he tore away across the camp.

'I'm going to hand in my resignation to Clancy,' he hissed.

'But what good will that do? It will only mean you'll have to do fatigues instead and Brennan will get his knife in you too.'

'And isn't that what I want?' he cried. 'You don't think I'm going to stop outside in freedom and leave poor Mick in there alone?'

I was on the point of asking him his definition of freedom, but I realized in time that he wasn't in a state to discuss the question philosophically, so I thought I had better accompany him. Clancy received us in a fatherly way; his conscience was obviously at him about having sent Mick to jail.

'Now don't do anything in a hurry, boy,' he said kindly. 'I spoke to the Commandant about it. It seems he admires Stewart a lot, but he has to do it for the sake of discipline.'

'Is that what you call discipline?' Matt asked bitterly. 'You can tell the Commandant from me that I'm resigning from the army as well. I wouldn't be mixed up with tyrants like ye.'

'Tyrants?' spluttered Clancy, getting red. 'Who are you calling tyrants?'

'And what the hell else are ye?' cried Matt. 'The English were gentlemen to ye.'

'Clear out!' cried Clancy. 'Clear out or I'll kick the ass off you, you ungrateful little pup!'

'Tyrant!' hissed Matt, turning purple.

'You young cur!' said Clancy. 'Wait till I tell your father about you!'

That evening I stood for a long time outside the prison window with Matt, talking to Mick. Mick had to raise himself on the bucket; he held onto the bars with both hands; he had the appearance of a real prisoner. The camp too looked like a place where people were free; in the dusk it looked big and complex and citified. Twenty yards away the prisoners on their evening strolls went round and round, and among them were the camp command, the Commandant, the Adjutant, and Clancy, not even giving a look in our direction. I had the greatest difficulty in keeping Matt from taking a fistful of stones and going round breaking windows to get himself arrested. I knew that wouldn't help. His other idea was that the three of us should resign from the army and conclude a separate peace with the British. That, as I pointed out, would be even worse. The great thing was to put the staff in the wrong by showing ourselves more loyal than they. I proposed to prepare a full statement of the position to be smuggled out to our friends at Brigade Headquarters outside. This idea rather appealed to Mick who, as I say, was very reasonable about most things.

I spent the evening after lock-up and a good part of the following morning on it. In the afternoon I went over to J with it. Brennan was distributing the mail and there were a couple of letters for Matt.

'Isn't there anything for Stewart?' he asked in disappointment.

'Stewart's letters will be sent to the staff hut,' growled Brennan.

'You mean you're not going to give the man his letters?' shouted Matt.

'I mean I don't know whether he's entitled to them or not,' said Brennan. 'That's a matter for the Commandant.'

Matt had begun a violent argument before I led him away. In the temper of the hut he could have been lynched. I wondered more than ever at the conservatism of revolutionaries.

'Come to the staff hut and we'll inquire ourselves,' I said. 'Brennan is probably only doing this out of pique.'

I should have gone alone, of course. The Adjutant was there with Clancy. He was a farmer's son from the Midlands, beef to the heels like a Mullingar heifer.

'Brennan says Mick Stewart isn't entitled to letters,' Matt squeaked to Clancy. 'Is that right?'

'Why wouldn't it be?' Clancy asked, jumping up and giving one truculent tug to his moustache, another to his waistcoat. Obviously he didn't know whether it was or not. With the new jail only just started, precedents were few.

'Whenever the English want to score off us they stop our letters and parcels,' I said. 'Surely to God ye could think up something more original.'

'Do you know who you're speaking to?' the Adjutant asked.

'No,' replied Matt before I could intervene. 'Nor don't want to. Ye know what ye can do with the letters.'

Mick, on the other hand, took the news coolly. He had apparently been thinking matters over during the night and planned his own campaign.

'I'm on hunger strike now,' he said with a bitter smile.

The moment he spoke I knew he had found the answer. It was what we politicals always did when the British tried to make ordinary convicts of us. And it put the staff in an impossible position. Steadily more and more they had allowed themselves to become more tyrannical than the British themselves, and Mick's hunger strike showed it up clearly. If Mick were to die on hunger strike – and I knew him well enough to know that he would, rather than give in – no one would ever take the staff seriously again as suffering Irish patriots. And even if they wished to let him die, they might find it difficult, because without our even having to approach the British directly we involved them as well. As our legal jailers they would hate to see Mick die on anyone else's hands. The British are very jealous of privileges like that.

At the same time I was too fond of Mick to want things to reach such a pass, and I decided to make a final appeal to Clancy. I also decided to do it alone, for I knew Matt was beyond reasonable discussion.

When I went into him at the store, Clancy lowered his head and pulled his moustache at me.

'You know about Mick Stewart?' I began.

'I know everything about him from the moment he was got,' shouted Clancy, putting his hand up to stop me. 'If you didn't hear of that incident remind me to tell you some time.'

This was a most unpromising beginning. The details of Mick's conception seemed to me beside the point.

'What are you going to do about it?' I asked.

'What do you think we're going to do about it?' he retorted, taking three steps back from me. 'What do you think we are? Soldiers or old women? Let the bugger starve!'

'That's grand,' I said, knowing I had him where I wanted

him. 'And what happens when we go on hunger strike and the British say: "Let the buggers starve"?'

'That has nothing at all to do with it.'

'Go on!' I said. 'By the way, I suppose ye considered forcible feeding?'

Then he said something very nasty, quite uncalled-for, which didn't worry me in the least because it was the way he always talked when he was his natural self, and I got on very well with Clancy's natural self.

'By the way,' I said, 'don't be too sure the British will let ye starve him. You seem to forget that you're still prisoners yourselves, and Stewart is their prisoner as much as yours. The English mightn't like the persecution of unfortunate Irish prisoners by people like you.'

Clancy repeated the uncalled-for remark, and I was suddenly filled with real pity for him. All that decent little man's life he had been suffering for Ireland, sacrificing his time and money and his little business, sleeping on the sofa and giving up his bed, selling raffle tickets, cycling miles in the dark to collect someone's subscription, and here was a young puppy taking the bread and water from his mouth.

That evening Matt and I stayed with Mick till the last whistle. You couldn't shift Matt from the window. He was on the verge of a breakdown. He had no one to coddle or be bullied by. Caliban without Prospero is a miserable spectacle.

But Clancy must have had a sleepless night. Next morning I found that Mick had already had a visit from the Adjutant. The proposal now was that Mick and Matt should come to my hut, and Mick could do his week's fatigues there – a mere formality so far as Q was concerned because anyone in that hut would do them for a sixpenny bit or five cigarettes. But no, Mick wouldn't agree to that either. He would accept nothing less than unconditional release, and even I felt that this was asking a lot of the staff.

But I was wrong. The staff had already given it up as a bad job. That afternoon we were summoned to the dining-hall 'to make arrangements about our immediate release' as the signaller told us – his idea of a joke. It looked like a company meeting. The staff sat round a table on the stage, Clancy wearing a collar and tie to show the importance of the occasion. The Commandant told us that the camp was faced with an unprecedented crisis. Clancy nodded three times, rapidly. They were the elected representatives of the men, and one man was deliberately defying them. Clancy crossed his legs, folded his arms tightly and looked searchingly through the audience as if looking for the criminal. They had no choice only to come back for fresh instructions.

It was a nice little meeting. Jack Costello, speaking from the hall, did a touching little piece about the hunger strike as the last weapon of free men against tyrants, told us that it should never be brought into disrepute, and said that if the man in question were released his loyal comrades would no doubt show what they thought of his conduct. Matt tried to put in a few words but was at once shouted down by his loyal comrades. Oh, a grand little meeting! Then I got up. I didn't quite know what to say because I didn't quite know what I thought. I had intended to say that within every conception of liberty there was the skeleton of a tyranny; that there were as many conceptions of liberty as there were human beings, and that the sort of liberty one man needed was not that which another might need. But somehow when I looked round me, I couldn't believe it. Instead, I said that there was no crisis, and that the staff were making mountains of principle out of molehills of friction. I wasn't permitted to get far. The Adjutant interrupted to say that what Mick was sentenced for couldn't be discussed by the meeting. Apparently it couldn't be discussed at all except by a Court of Appeal which couldn't be set up until the Republic proclaimed in 1916 was re-established, or some such nonsense. Listening to the Adjutant always gave me the impression of having taken a powerful sleeping-pill; after a while your hold on reality began to weaken and queer dissociated sentences began to run through your mind. I went out, deciding it was better to walk it off. Matt and I met outside the jail and waited till Kenefick came to release the prisoner. He did it in complete silence. Apparently orders were that we were to be sent to Coventry.

That suited me fine. The three of us were now together in Q and I knew from old experience that anyone in Q would sell his old mother for a packet of cigarettes. But all the same I was puzzled and depressed. Puzzled because I couldn't clarify what I had really meant to say when I got up to speak at the meeting, because I couldn't define what I really meant by liberty; depressed because if there was no liberty which I could define then equally there was no escape. I remained awake for hours that night thinking of it. Beyond the restless searchlights which stole in through every window and swept the hut till it was bright as day I could feel the wide fields of Ireland all round me, but even the wide fields of Ireland were not wide enough. Choice was an illusion. Seeing that a man can never really get out of jail, the great thing is to ensure that he gets into the biggest possible one with the largest possible range of modern amenities.

The Holy Door

Polly Donegan and Nora Lawlor met every morning after eight o'clock Mass. They were both good-living girls; indeed, they were among the best girls in town. Nora had a round soft face and great round wondering eyes. She was inquisitive, shy, and a dreamer — an awkward combination. Her father, a builder called Jerry Lawlor, had been Vice-Commandant of the Volunteers during the Troubles.

Polly was tall, with coal-black hair, a long, proud, striking face, and an air of great calm and resolution. As they went down the hill from the church she saluted everyone with an open pleasant smile and accepted whatever invitations she got. Nora went through the torments of the damned whenever anyone invited her anywhere; curiosity and timidity combined made her visualize every consequence of accepting or not accepting, down to the last detail.

Now Nora, with that peculiar trait in her make-up, had a knack which Polly found very disconcerting of bringing the conversation round to the facts of life. To Nora the facts of life were the ultimate invitation; acceptance meant never-ending embarrassment, refusal a curiosity unsatisfied till death. While she struggled to put her complex in words Polly adopted a blank and polite air and without the least effort retreated into her own thoughts of what they should have for dinner.

'You're not listening to a word I say,' Nora said on a note of complaint.

'Oh, I am, Nora, I am,' Polly said impatiently. 'But I'll have to be rushing or I'll be late for breakfast.'

Nora could see that Polly wasn't even interested in the facts of life. She wondered a lot about that. Was Polly natural? Was it possible not to be curious? Was she only acting sly like all the Donegans? Nora had thought so long about God's inscrutable purpose in creating mankind in two sexes that she could hardly see the statue of a saint without wondering what he'd be like without his clothes. That was no joke in our church, where there are statues inside the door and in each of the side-chapels and along the columns of the arcade. It makes the church quite gay, but it was terrible temptation to Nora, who found it hard not to see them all like Greek statues, and whatever it was about their faces and gestures they seemed worse like that than any Greek divinities. To the truly pious mind there is something appalling in the idea of St Aloysius Gonzaga without his clothes.

That particular notion struck Polly as the height of nonsense.

'Wisha, Nora,' she said with suppressed fury, 'what things you think about!'

'But after all,' retorted Nora with a touch of fire, 'they must have had bodies like the rest of us.'

'Why then indeed, Nora, they'd be very queer without them,' said Polly serenely, and it was clear to Nora that she hadn't a glimmer. 'Anyway, what has it to do with us?'

'You might find it has a lot to do with you when you get married,' said Nora darkly.

'Ah, well, it'll never worry me so,' said Polly confidently.

'Why, Polly? Won't you ever get married?'

'What a thing I'd do!' said Polly.

'But why, Polly?' asked Nora eagerly, hoping that at last she might discover some point where Polly's fastidiousness met her own.

'Ah,' Polly sighed, 'I could never imagine myself married. No matters how fond of them you'd be. Like Susie. I always hated sharing a room with Susie. She was never done talking.'

'Oh, if talking was all that was in it!' exclaimed Nora with a dark brightness like a smile.

'I think talking is the worst of all, Nora,' Polly said firmly. 'I can't imagine anything worse.'

'There's a shock in store for you if you do marry,' said Nora darkly.

'What sort of shock, Nora?' asked Polly.

'Oh, of course, you can't even describe it,' said Nora fretfully. 'No one will even tell you. People you knew all your life go on as if you were only a child and couldn't be told.'

'Do they really, Nora?' Polly said with a giggle, inspired less by thought of what the mystery could be than by that of Nora's inquisitiveness brought to a full stop for once.

'If you get married before me will you tell me?' Nora asked.

'Oh, I will to be sure, girl,' said Polly in the tone of one promising to let her know when the coalman came.

'But I mean everything, Polly,' Nora said earnestly.

'Oh, why wouldn't I, Nora?' Polly cried impatiently, showing that Nora's preoccupation with the facts of life struck her as being uncalled-for. 'Anyway, you're more likely to be married than I am. Somehow I never had any inclination for it.'

It was clear that her sister's garrulity had blighted some man's chance of Polly.

2

Charlie Cashman was a great friend of Nora's father and a regular visitor to her home. He had been her father's Commandant during the Troubles. He owned the big hardware store in town and this he owed entirely to his good national record. He and his mother had never got on, for she hated the Volunteers as she hated the books he read; she looked on him as a flighty fellow and had determined early in his life that the shop would go to her second son, John Joe. As Mrs Cashman was a woman who had never known what it was not to have her own way, Charlie had resigned himself to this, and after the Troubles, cleared out and worked as a shop assistant in Asragh. But then old John Cashman died, having never in his lifetime contradicted his wife, and his will was found to be nothing but a contradiction. It seemed that he had always been a violent nationalist and admired culture and hated John Joe, and Charlie, as in the novels, got every damn thing, even his mother being left in the house only on sufferance.

Charlie was a good catch and there was no doubt of his liking for Nora, but somehow Nora couldn't bear him. He was an airy, excitable man with a plump, sallow, wrinkled face that always looked as if it needed shaving, a pair of keen grey eyes in slits under bushy brows; hair on his cheekbones, hair in his ears, hair even in his nose. He wore a dirty old tweed suit and a cap. Nora couldn't stand him – even with his clothes on. She told herself that it was the cleft in his chin, which someone had once told her betokened a sensual nature, but it was really the thought of all the hair. It made him look so animal!

Besides, there was something sly and double-meaning about him. He was, by town standards, a very well-read man. Once he found Nora reading St Francis de Sales and asked her if she'd ever read *Romeo and Juliet* with such a knowing air that he roused her dislike even further. She gave him a cold and penetrating look which should have crushed him but didn't – he was so thick.

'As a matter of fact I have,' she said steadily, just to show him that true piety did not exclude a study of the grosser aspects of life.

'What did you think of it?' he asked.

'I thought it contained a striking moral lesson,' said Nora.

'Go on!' Charlie exclaimed with a grin. 'What was that, Nora?'

'It showed where unrestrained passion can carry people,' she said.

'Ah, I wouldn't notice that,' said Charlie. 'Your father and myself were a bit wild too, in our time.'

Her father, a big, pop-eyed, open-gobbed man, looked at them both and said nothing, but he knew from their tone that they were sparring across him and he wanted to know more about it. That night after Charlie had gone he looked at Nora with a terrible air.

'What's that book Charlie Cashman was talking about?' he asked. 'Did I read that?'

'*Romeo and Juliet*?' she said with a start. 'It's there on the shelf behind you. In the big Shakespeare.'

Jerry took down the book and looked even more astonished.

'That's a funny way to write a book,' he said. 'What is it about?'

She told him the story as well as she could, with a slight tendency to make Friar Laurence the hero, and her father looked more pop-eyed than ever. He had a proper respect for culture.

'But they were married all right?' he asked at last.

'They were,' said Nora. 'Why?'

'Ah, that was a funny way to take him up so,' her father said cantankerously. ' 'Tisn't as if there was anything wrong in it.' He went to the foot of the stairs with his hands in his trouser pockets while Nora watched him with a hypnotized air. She knew what he was thinking of. 'Mind,' he said, 'I'm not trying to force him on you, but there's plenty of girls in this town would be glad of your chance.'

That was all he said but Nora wanted no chances. She would have preferred to die in the arena like a Christian martyr sooner than marry a man with so much hair. She never even gave Charlie the opportunity of proposing, though she knew her father and he had discussed it between themselves.

And then, to her utter disgust, Charlie transferred his attentions to Polly, whom he had met at her house. Of course, her disgust had nothing to do with jealousy of Polly. Mainly it was inspired by the revelation it afforded of masculine character, particularly of Charlie's. Sensual, flighty, he had not had the decency to remain a celibate for the rest of his life; he hadn't threatened suicide, hadn't even to be taken away for a long holiday by his friends. He merely cut his losses as though she were a type of car he couldn't afford and took the next cheapest.

It left her depressed about human nature in general. Only too well had her father gauged the situation. Not only did the Donegans go all-out to capture Charlie but Polly herself seemed quite pleased. After all she had said against marriage, this struck Nora as sly. In more judicious moments she knew she was not being quite fair to Polly. The truth was probably that Polly, being a good-natured, dutiful girl, felt if she were to marry at all, she should do so in such a way as to oblige her family. She did not mind the hair and had a genuine liking for Charlie. She was a modest girl who made no claim to brains; she never even knew which of the two parties was the government of the moment, and Charlie could explain it all to her in the most interesting way. To her he seemed a man of really gigantic intellect, and listening to him was like listening to a great preacher.

Yet, even admitting all this, Nora thought her conduct pretty strange. The Donegans were all sly. It caused a certain coldness between the two girls, but Polly was self-centred and hard-hearted and Nora got the worst of that.

3

Like all young brides-to-be, Polly was full of plans. When Charlie asked where they should go on their honeymoon she looked troubled.

'Ah, 'twould cost too much,' she said in her tangential way.

'What would cost too much, girl?' Charlie replied recklessly. 'Never mind what it costs. Where do you want to go?'

'Lourdes?' Polly asked, half as a question. 'Is that far, Charlie?'

'Lourdes,' repeated Charlie in bewilderment. 'What do you want to go to Lourdes for?'

'Oh, only for the sake of the pilgrimage,' said Polly. 'You never read *The Life of Bernadette*, Charlie?'

'Never,' said Charlie promptly, in dread he was going to be compelled to read it. 'We'll go to Lourdes.'

It was all arranged when one day Polly and Nora met in the street. Nora was self-conscious; she was thinking of all the things she had said of Charlie to Polly and certain they had got back (they hadn't, but Nora judged by herself).

'Where are ye going for the honeymoon?' she asked.

'You'd never guess,' replied Polly joyously.

'Where?' Nora asked, her eyes beginning to pop.

'Lourdes, imagine!'

'Lourdes?' cried Nora aghast. 'But didn't you know?'

'Know what, Nora?' Polly asked, alarmed in her turn. 'Don't tell me 'tis forbidden.'

' 'Tisn't that at all but 'tis unlucky,' said Nora breathlessly. 'I only knew one girl that did it and she died inside a year.'

'Oh, Law, Nora,' Polly cried with bitter disappointment, 'how is it nobody told me that, or what sort of people do they have in those travel agencies?'

'I suppose they took it for granted you'd know,' said Nora.

'How *could* I know, Nora?' Polly cried despairingly. 'Even Charlie doesn't know, and he's supposed to be an educated man.'

Away she rushed to challenge Charlie and they had their first big row. Charlie was now reconciled to Lourdes by the prospect of a few days in Paris, and he stamped and fumed about Nora Lawlor and her blasted pishrogues, but you did not catch a prudent girl like Polly risking fortune and happiness by defying the will of God, and a few days before the wedding everything was cancelled. They went to Connemara instead.

They arrived there on a wet evening and Polly said dismally that it wasn't in the least like what she expected. This was not the only thing that failed to come up to expectations, nor was hers the only disappointment. She had brought a little statue of the Blessed Virgin and put it on the table by her bed. Then she said her night prayers and undressed. She was rather surprised at the way Charlie looked at her but not really upset. She was exhausted after the journey and remarked to Charlie on the comfort of the bed. 'Oh,' she said with a yawn, 'I don't think there's anything in the world like bed.' At this Charlie gave her a wolfish grin, not like any grin she'd ever seen before, and it filled her with alarm. 'Oh, Charlie, what did I say?' she asked. Charlie didn't reply, which was still more alarming; he got into bed beside her and she gave a loud gasp that could be heard right through the hotel.

For the rest of the night her brain, not usually retentive of ideas, had room only for one. 'Can it be? Is it possible? Why did nobody tell me?' She kept herself from flying out of the room in hysterics only by repeating aspirations like 'Jesus, mercy! Mary, help!' She thought of all the married women she had known from her mother on – fat, pious, good-natured women you saw every morning at Mass – and wondered if they had lived all those years with such a secret in their hearts. Now she knew exactly what Nora had been trying to find out and why no one had ever told her. It was something that couldn't be told, only endured. One faint hope remained; that after years she might get used to it as the others seemed to have done. But then it all began again and she muttered aspirations to herself loud enough for Charlie to hear, and knew she could never, never get used to it; and when it was over a bitter anger smouldered in her against all the nonsense that had been written about it by old gasbags like Shakespeare. 'Oh, what liars they are!' she thought, wishing she could just lay her hands on one of them for five minutes. 'What liars!'

The day after they returned from the honeymoon Nora called. She had managed to bottle her curiosity just so far. Charlie was in the shop and she smiled shyly at him. Polly and herself sat in the best room overlooking the Main Street and had their tea. Nora noticed with satisfaction that she looked a bit haggard. Then Nora lit a cigarette and sat back.

'And what does it feel like to be married?' she asked with a smile.

'Oh, all right, Nora,' Polly replied, though for a moment her face looked more haggard than before.

'And how do you find Charlie?'

'Oh, much like anyone else, I suppose,' Polly said doubtfully, and her eyes strayed in the direction of the window.

'And is that all you're going to tell us?' Nora went on with a nervous laugh.

'Oh, whatever do you mean, Nora?' Polly asked indignantly.

'I thought you were going to advise me,' Nora said lightly, though with a growing feeling that there was nothing to be got out of Polly.

'Oh, Law, Nora,' Polly said with a distraught air, 'I don't think it can ever be right to talk about things like that.'

Nora knew she would never get anything out of Polly. She would never get anything out of anybody. They were all the same. They went inside and the door closed behind them for ever. She felt like crying.

'Was it as bad as that?' she asked with chagrin.

'I think I'd sooner not talk about it at all, Nora,' Polly said firmly. She bowed her head; her smooth forehead became fenced with wrinkles and a second chin began to peep from beneath the first.

4

Charlie's shop was on Main Street; a store like a cave, with buckets and spades hanging and stacked at either side of the opening. When you went in there was hardware on your right and the general store on the left. Charlie looked after the hardware and Polly and a girl assistant after the rest. Charlie's end of it was really well run; there wasn't a bit of agricultural machinery for miles around that he didn't know the workings of and for which, at a pinch, he couldn't produce at least the substitute for a spare part.

Polly wasn't brilliant in that way, but she was conscientious and polite. In every way she was all a wife should be; obliging, sweet-tempered, good-humoured, and so modest that she wouldn't even allow Charlie to put on the light while she dressed for Mass on a winter morning. Mrs Cashman had always had a great selection of holy pictures but Polly had brought a whole gallery with her. There was also a Lourdes clock which played the Lourdes hymn at the Angelus hours – very soothing and devotional – but at the same time Charlie was just the least bit disappointed.

He was disappointed and he couldn't say why. 'Romeo, Romeo, wherefore art thou, Romeo?' he would suddenly find himself declaiming about nothing at all. Italian women were probably different. No doubt it was the sun! He was a restless man and he had hoped marriage would settle him. It hadn't settled him. When he had closed the shop for the night and should have been sitting upstairs with his book and his pipe, the longing would suddenly seize him to go out to Johnny Desmond's pub instead. He would walk in and out the hall and peer up and down the street till the restlessness became too much for him. It was all very disconcerting. Sometimes for consolation he went back to the shop, switched on the lamp over his desk, and took out the copy of his father's will. This was the will from which he had expected nothing and which gave him everything. He read it through again with a reverent expression. He had always liked the will; admired its massive style, the way it carefully excluded all possibility of misunderstanding; it had given him a new respect for lawyers; indeed, in its own way it was as powerful as Shakespeare.

One murky, gloomy afternoon when business had stopped his mother came in and found him at it. He gave her a sly grin. She was a cranky, crafty, monotonous old woman, twisted with rheumatics and malice.

'I was just saying my office,' he said.

'Oh, I see what you're at,' she said with resignation. 'I saw it long ago.'

'Fine, devotional reading!' said Charlie, slapping a hairy paw on the will.

'Go on, you blasphemous bosthoon!' she said without rancour. 'You were always too smart for your poor slob of a brother. But take care you wouldn't be keeping the bed warm for him yet!'

'What's that you say?' asked Charlie, startled.

'God spoke first,' intoned his mother. 'Many a better cake didn't rise.'

She went out, banging the door behind her, and left Charlie gasping, naked to the cruel day. The will had lost it magical power. There was one clause in it to which he had never paid attention – there never had been any reason why he should do so – entailing the shop on his children, and, failing those, on John Joe's. And John Joe had four with another coming while Charlie still had none.

Another man only a year married wouldn't have given it a thought but Charlie wasn't that kind. The man was a born worrier. With his hands in his pockets he paced moodily to the shop door and stood there, leaning against the jamb, his legs crossed and his cap pulled down over his eyes.

His mother read him like a book. The least thing was enough to set him off. At the first stroke of the Angelus he put up the shutters and ate his supper. Then he lit his pipe and strolled to the hall door for a look up and down the Main Street on the offchance of seeing somebody or something. He never did, but it was as well to make sure. Then he returned to the kitchen, his feet beginning to drag as they usually did before he set out for Johnny Desmond's. It was their way of indicating that they weren't moving in the right direction. His mother had gone to the chapel and Polly was sitting by the table under the window. Charlie took a deep breath, removed his hands from his pockets, raised his head, and squared his shoulders.

'Well,' he said briskly, 'I might as well take a little turn.'

'Wisha, you might as well, Charlie,' Polly replied without resentment.

It was only what she always said, but in Charlie's state of depression it sounded like a dead key on a piano. He felt it was a hard thing that a married man of a year's standing had no inclination to stop at home and that his wife had no inclination to make him. Not that she could have made him even if she had tried but he felt that a little persuasion wouldn't have been out of place.

'The mother wasn't talking to you?' he asked keenly.

'No, Charlie,' Polly said in surprise. 'What would she talk to me about?'

'Oh, nothing in particular ... Only she was remarking that you were a long time about having a family,' he added with a touch of reproach.

'Oh, Law, Charlie,' Polly cried, 'wasn't that a very queer thing for her to say?'

'Was it, I wonder?' Charlie said as though to himself but giving her a sideway glance.

'But Charlie, you don't think I won't have children, do you?' she exclaimed.

'Oh, no, no, no,' Charlie replied hastily, in dread he might have said too much. 'But 'twould suit her fine if you hadn't. Then she'd have the place for John Joe's children.'

'But how would John Joe's children get it?' asked Polly. 'Didn't your father leave it to you?'

'To me and my children,' said Charlie. 'If I hadn't children 'twould go to John Joe's.'

'Oh, Law, Charlie, isn't that a great worry to you?'

'Well, it is, a bit,' Charlie conceded, scratching his poll. 'I put a lot of work into the place. No one likes working for another man's family. You wouldn't see a doctor?'

'I'd have to ask Father Ring first.'

That upset Charlie again. He nearly told her it was Father Ring she should have married, but remembered in time that she'd be bound to confess it. There's nothing a good-living woman likes so much as confessing her husband's sins.

5

Charlie's remarks brought Polly for the first time up against the facts of life. This made her very thoughtful, but it was a week before should could even bring herself to discuss it with Nora. It was a subject you could only discuss with a woman, and an intellectual woman at that, and Nora was the only intellectual woman Polly knew.

Nora was not inclined to treat it as seriously as Charlie had done. According to her there was a lot of chance in it. Some people went on for years before they had a child; others didn't even wait for their time to be up. It was quite shocking when you came to think of it, but somehow Polly never did get round to thinking of it. If you were really in trouble, there was always the Holy Door. Johnny Fleming the barrister and his wife had been married ten years without having children, and they had made the pilgrimage to the Holy Door, and now people were beginning to say it was about time they made another to shut off the power.

'I suppose I could go next year if I had to,' said Polly doubtfully.

'You'll have to go this year if you're going at all,' said Nora. 'It's only opened once in seven years.'

'Seven years!' cried Polly. 'Oh, I could never wait as long as that.'

'It would be too dangerous anyway,' said Nora. 'There was a woman up our road waited till she was thirty-eight to have a child, and she died.'

'Oh, Law!' cried Polly, a little peeved. 'I suppose 'tis wrong to be criticizing, but really, the Lord's ways are very peculiar.'

So back she went to Charlie with her story. Charlie screwed up his face as though he were hard of hearing, a favourite trick of his whenever he wanted to gain time. He wanted to gain it now.

'Where did you say?' he asked searchingly.

'Rome,' repeated Polly.

'Rome?' echoed Charlie with a mystified air. 'And what did you say you wanted to go to Rome for?'

'It's the pilgrimage to the Holy Door,' said Polly. 'You wouldn't know about that?' she asked in the trustful tone she used to indicate the respect she had for his learning.

'No,' replied Charlie doubtfully, playing up to the part of the well-informed husband. 'What sort of door?'

'A holy door.'

'A holy door?'

''Tis only opened once in seven years, and 'tis good for people that want families,' prompted Polly hopefully.

'Is that so?' asked Charlie gravely. 'Who told you about that?'

'Nora Lawlor.'

'Tut, tut, tut,' clucked Charlie impatiently, 'ah, I wouldn't say there would be any truth in that, Polly.'

'Oh, Law, Charlie,' she cried in ringing tones, outraged at his lack of faith, 'you surely don't think the Flemings would go all that way unless there was something in it?'

'Oh, no, no, no, I dare say not,' Charlie said hastily, seeing that any further objections he made were likely to be reported back to Father Ring. 'I'm afraid I couldn't get away, though.'

'Well, I'll have to get away, Charlie,' Polly said with quiet decision. 'It might be too late if I left it for another seven years. Nora says 'tis very dangerous.'

'And a hell of a lot of danger that one will ever be in!' snapped Charlie fierily.

His bad temper did not last long. This was an excuse for an outing, and Charlie loved an outing. He had never been farther than London before; Paris staggered him; he experimented with green drinks, pink drinks, and yellow drinks with the satisfied expression of a child in a pantry; and while the train passed through the Alps in the late evening he wedged himself in the corridor with his elbows on the rail, humming 'Home to Our Mountains', while tears of excitement poured down his hairy cheeks. He couldn't forget that he was going to the homeland of Romeo and Juliet.

He quickly made friends with the other two occupants of the carriage, a fat Dutchman in shirtsleeves who ate sausages and embraced the woman beside him who he said was his wife. The sight was too gross for Polly and she went and stood in the corridor but not to look at the scenery.

'Isn't she beautiful?' said the Dutchman, stroking his companion affectionately under the chin.

'Grand! grand!' agreed Charlie enthusiastically, nodding and smiling encouragement to the woman, who couldn't speak English and to all appearances didn't know much of any other language either.

'That's a nice-looking girl with you,' said the Dutchman. 'Who is she?'

'Polly?' said Charlie, looking at the gloomy figure in the corridor. 'Oh, that's the wife.'

'Whose wife?' asked the Dutchman.

'Mine,' said Charlie.

'And don't you love her?'

'Love her?' echoed Charlie, giving another peep out. 'I'm cracked on her, of course.'

'Then why don't you make love to her?' asked the Dutchman in surprise. 'Women can't have enough of it. Look at this!'

'Ah, mine wouldn't like it,' said Charlie in alarm. 'In Ireland we don't go in much for that sort of thing.'

'And what do you go in for?'

'Well,' said Charlie doubtfully, seeing that he didn't quite know, himself – apart from politics, which didn't sound right – 'we're more in the sporting line; horses and dogs, you know.'

'Ah,' said the Dutchman earnestly, 'you can't beat women.'

Charlie went out to Polly, who was leaning with her back to the compartment and with a brooding look on her face.

'Charlie, how do they do it?' she asked in a troubled voice. 'Wouldn't you think the woman would drop dead with shame? I suppose they're Protestants, are they, Charlie?'

'I dare say, I dare say,' said Charlie, thinking it was better not to try and explain.

6

It was a great outing and it lasted Charlie in small talk for a month. The grapes like gooseberries, and from nightfall on every little café with soprano or tenor or baritone bawling away about love – *amore, mio cuore, traditore* – you could see where Juliet got it. But they weren't there long enough for Polly to be infected, and all the wonders she brought back was her astonishment at the way the men in St Peter's pinched her bottom. 'Your what, Polly?' the neighbours asked in surprise. 'My bottom,' repeated Polly incredulously. 'Would you believe it?'

After that, Morgan, the wit of Johnny Desmond's pub, began dropping nasty remarks about doors of one sort and another, while old Mrs Cashman, getting over her alarm at the possibility of divine intervention, declared loudly that it would be a poor lookout for a woman like her to be relying on a son who had to take his wife to Rome. It didn't take a miracle to start John Joe's wife off, for the poor wretch had only to look at her.

But Polly, to give her her due, was every bit as upset as Charlie. Sixty pounds odd the pilgrimage had cost, and they had absolutely nothing to show for it. If the Holy Door couldn't do a thing like that it couldn't be so holy after all. She scolded Nora Lawlor a lot over her bad advice.

'But after all, Polly,' Nora said reasonably, 'you mustn't expect too much. It might be something mental.'

'Oh, how could it, Nora?' Polly cried in a fury. 'What a thing to say!'

'But why not?' asked Nora with a touch of asperity. 'If you didn't feel attracted to Charlie—'

'Oh,' said Polly vaguely and guardedly but with a dim

comprehension dawning in her eyes, 'would that make a difference?'

'It might make all the difference in the world, Polly,' Nora said severely. 'After all, there was Kitty Daly. She was married eight years without having a family, and one night she pretended to herself that her husband was Rudolph Valentino, and everything was all right.'

'Rudolph Valentino?' said Polly. 'Who's he?'

'He was a film actor,' said Nora.

'But why would she do that?'

'Well, I suppose he was a nice-looking man, and you know what sort Jerome Daly is.'

'Would there be a picture of that fellow that I could see?' asked Polly.

'I wouldn't say so,' replied Nora. 'Anyway, he's dead now, so I suppose it wouldn't be right. But, of course, there are plenty of others just as nice-looking.'

'Oh, I don't think it could ever be right,' cried Polly with a petulant toss of her head. She was feeling very sorry for herself. She knew quite well that that sly thing, Nora, was trying to worm out of her what Charlie really did to her and she was torn asunder between the need for revealing something and the desire not to reveal anything at all. 'I'm sure Father Ring would say it was wrong.'

'I don't see why he would,' Nora said coolly. 'After all, it was done with a good purpose.'

Polly had no reply to that, for she knew the importance of doing things with a good purpose, but at the same time the temptation lingered. The following Saturday evening she went to confession to Father Ring. Her sins didn't take long to tell. They were never what you'd call major ones.

'Father,' she said when she had done, 'I want to ask your advice.'

'What about, my child?' asked Father Ring.

'It's my husband, Father,' said Polly. 'You see, we have no children, and I know it's a terrible worry to him, so I went on the pilgrimage to the Holy Door but it didn't do me any good.'

'Go on,' said Father Ring.

'So a friend of mine was telling me about another woman that was in the same position. It seems she imagined her husband was Rudolph Valentino.'

'Who was he?'

'Some sort of fellow on the pictures.'

'But what made her think he was her husband?' asked Father Ring with a puzzled frown.

'Oh, she didn't think it,' said Polly in distress. 'She only pretended. It seems he was a very nice-looking fellow and her husband is an insignificant little man ... Of course, I could understand that,' she added candidly. 'My husband is a very good fellow, but somehow he doesn't look right.'

'Is it Charlie?' exclaimed Father Ring, so astonished that he broke the tone of decent anonymity in which the discussion was being conducted. 'Sure, Charlie is a grand-looking man.'

'Oh, would you think so?' asked Polly with real interest. 'Of course I might be wrong. But anyway, this woman had a child after.'

'What did she call him?' asked Father Ring.

'I don't know, Father. Why? Does it make any difference?'

'No. I was just wondering.'

'But tell me, Father, would that ever be right?' asked Polly.

'Ah, I don't say there would be anything wrong about it,' said Father Ring, pulling aside the curtain before the confessional and peeping out into the darkened church. 'Of course she did it with a good object.'

'That's what my friend said,' said Polly, amazed at the intellect of that little gligeen of a girl.

'Provided, of course, she didn't get any pleasure from it,' Father Ring added hastily. 'If she got carnal pleasure out of it that would be a different thing.'

'Oh!' exclaimed Polly, aghast. 'You don't think she'd do that?'

'What I mean,' the priest explained patiently, 'is more than the natural pleasure.'

'The natural pleasure?' repeated Polly with a stunned air.

'However,' said Father Ring hastily, 'I don't think you're in much danger of that.'

It was shortly after this that Charlie began to notice a change in the atmosphere in Johnny Desmond's. Charlie was very sensitive to atmosphere. First Morgan passed a remark about Polly and the new teacher, Carmody. Now, Carmody was a relative of Father Ring's, as has been said, a good-looking plausible Kerryman who put on great airs with the women. Charlie greeted the remark with a sniff and a laugh and was almost on the point of telling how Polly wouldn't let him switch on the light while she dressed for Mass. Then he began to wonder. The remark had stuck. The next time Polly's name was mentioned in connexion with Carmody he scowled. It was clear that something was going on and that he was the victim. He couldn't bear the thought of that. It might be that in her innocence Polly was being indiscreet. On the other hand it might well be that like many another woman before her, she was only letting on to be innocent to get the chance of being indiscreet. A man could never tell. He went home feeling very upset.

He strode in the hall and snapped a command to Polly, who was sitting in the darkness over the range. She rose in surprise and followed him meekly up the stairs. In the sitting-room he lit the gas and stooped to look up under the mantel as though to see if the burner was broken. Like all worriers Charlie considered nothing beneath him.

'Sit down,' he said curtly over his shoulder.

'Oh, Law, what is it at all, Charlie?' Polly asked nervously.

Charlie turned and stood on the hearthrug, his legs apart like buttresses, his cap drawn down over his eyes, and seemed as if he were studying her through his hairy cheekbones. It was a matter that required study. He had no precedent for inquiring whether or not Polly had been unfaithful to him.

'Tell me, Polly,' he said at last in a reasonable tone which seemed to suit the part, 'did I do anything to you?'

'Oh, whatever do you mean, Charlie?' she asked in bewilderment. 'What could you do to me?'

'That's just what I'd like to know,' said Charlie, nodding sagaciously. 'What I did out of the way.'

'Oh, Charlie,' she exclaimed in alarm, 'what a thing to say to me! I never said you did anything out of the way.'

'I'm glad to hear it,' said Charlie, nodding again and looking away across the room at the picture of a sailing-ship in distress. 'I suppose you don't know the new teacher in the school?' he added with the innocent air of a cross-examining lawyer.

'Is it Mr Carmody?' she asked, giving herself away at once by the suspicion of a blush.

'Aha, I see you do,' said Charlie.

'I met him a couple of times with Mrs MacCann,' Polly explained patiently. 'What about him?'

'Now is that all?' Charlie asked accusingly. 'You might as well tell me the truth now and not have me drag it out of you.'

'Oh, what do you mean?' cried Polly, sitting erect with indignation. 'What would you drag out of me? I don't know what's coming over you at all, Charlie.'

'Hold on now, hold on!' Charlie said commandingly, raising one hand for silence. 'Just sit where you are for a minute.' He put his hands behind his back, tilted forward on his toes and studied his feet for a moment. 'Do you know,' he added gravely, barely raising his head to fix her with his eyes, 'that 'tis all over the town that you and Carmody are carrying on behind my back? Isn't that a nice thing to have said about your wife?' he added, raising his voice.

Up to that moment he had only partly believed in her guilt, but he no longer had any doubt when he saw how she changed colour. It was partly anger, partly shame.

'Oh,' she cried in a fury, tossing her handsome black head, 'the badness of people! This is all Nora Lawlor's fault. Father Ring would never repeat a thing like that.'

'Father Ring?' exclaimed Charlie with a start, seeing that, whatever her crime was, it was already public property. 'What has he to do with it?'

'I see it all now,' Polly cried dramatically with a large wave of her arm. 'I should never have trusted her. I might have known she'd bell it all over the town.'

'What would she bell?' snapped Charlie impatiently. At the

very best of times Polly was not what you'd call lucid, but whenever anything happened to upset her, every joint in her mind flew asunder.

'She said,' explained Polly earnestly, wagging a long arm at him, 'that Kitty Daly had a child after imagining her husband was Rudolph Valentino.'

'Rudolph who?' asked Charlie with a strained air.

'You wouldn't know him,' replied Polly impatiently. 'He's an old fellow on the pictures. He's dead now.'

'And what has he to do with Carmody?' Charlie asked anxiously.

'He has nothing to do with Carmody,' shouted Polly, enraged at his stupidity.

'Well, go on, woman, go on!' said Charlie, his face screwed up in a black knot as he tried to disentangle the confusion she had plunged him in.

'Oh, I know it couldn't be wrong, Charlie,' Polly said positively, flying off at another tangent. 'I asked Father Ring myself was it wrong for her.'

'Wrong for who?' snarled Charlie, beside himself.

'Kitty Daly, of course,' shouted Polly.

'Christ Almighty!' groaned Charlie. 'Do you want to drive me mad?'

'But when you won't listen to me!' Polly cried passionately. 'And Father Ring said there was no harm in it so long as she was doing it for a good purpose and didn't get any pleasure out of it ... Though indeed,' she added candidly, 'I'm sure I have no idea what pleasure she could get out of it.'

'Ah, botheration!' shouted Charlie, shaking his fists at her. 'What goings-on you have about Rudolph Valentino! Don't you see I'm demented with all this hugger-mugger? What did you do then, woman?'

'I went to the pictures,' replied Polly with an aggrieved air.

'You went to the pictures with Carmody?' asked Charlie encouragingly, only too willing to compound for an infidelity with an indiscretion.

'Oh, what a thing I'd do!' cried Polly in a perfect tempest of indignation. 'Who said I went to the pictures with Mr Carmody? This town is full of liars. I went with Nora, of course.'

'Well?' asked Charlie.

'Well,' Polly continued in a more reasonable tone, 'I thought all the old men in the pictures were terrible, Charlie. How people can bear the sight of them night after night I do not know. And as we were coming out Nora asked me wasn't there any man at all I thought was good-looking, and I said: "Nora," I said, "I always liked Mr Carmody's appearance." "Oh, did you?" said Nora. "I did, Nora," said I. Now that,' said Polly flatly, bringing her palm down on her knee, 'was all that either of us said; and, of course, I might be wrong about his appearance, though I always thought he kept himself very nicely; but anyone that says I went to the pictures with him, Charlie, all I can say is that they have no conscience. Absolutely no conscience.'

Charlie stared at her for a moment in stupefaction. For that one moment he wondered at his own folly in ever thinking that Polly would have it in her to carry on with a man and in thinking that any man would try to carry on with her. *Amore, mio cuore, traditore,* he thought despairingly. Quite clearly Italian women must be different. And then the whole thing began to dawn on him and he felt himself suffocating with rage.

'And do you mean to tell me,' he asked incredulously, 'that you went to Father Ring and asked him could you pretend that I was Charlie Carmody?'

'Rudolph Valentino, Charlie,' corrected Polly. 'It was Nora Lawlor who suggested Mr Carmody ... You don't think it makes any difference?' she added hastily, terrified that she might unwittingly have drifted into mortal sin.

'You asked Father Ring could you pretend that I was Rudolph Valentino?' repeated Charlie frantically.

'Oh, surely Charlie,' Polly said, brushing this aside as mere trifling, 'you don't think I'd do it without finding out whether 'twas a sin or not?'

'God Almighty!' cried Charlie, turning to the door. 'I'm the laughing-stock of the town!'

'Oh, you think too much about what people say of you,'

Polly said impatiently. 'What need you care what they say so long as 'tis for a good object?'

'Good object!' cried Charlie bitterly. 'I know the object I'd like to lay my hands on this minute. It's that Nora Lawlor with her cesspool of a mind. By God, I'd wring her bloody neck!'

7

That was nothing to what Nora did later. Somebody, Charlie discovered, had put round the story that it was really his fault and not Polly's that they had no children. Of course, that might well have been a misconception of Polly's own, because he learned from a few words she dropped that she thought his mother was a witch and was putting spells on her. A girl who would believe that was quite capable of blaming it on the butcher's boy. But the obvious malice identified the story as Nora's. The Carmody business was only a flea-bite to it, because it lowered him in the estimation of everybody. Morgan made great play with it. And it was clever because Charlie was in no position to prove it a lie. Worst of all, he doubted himself. He was a nervous man; the least thing set him off; and for weeks and weeks he worried till he almost convinced himself that Nora was right, that he wasn't like other men. God had heaped so many burdens on him that this was all he could expect.

Now, the Cashmans had a maid called Molly O'Regan, a country girl with a rosy, laughing, good-natured face and a shrill penetrating voice. She was one of the few people Charlie knew who were not afraid of his mother, and in his bachelor days when she brought him his shaving-water of a morning, she had always leaned in the door and shown him just enough of herself to interest a half-wakened man. 'Come in, girl,' he would whisper, 'come in and shut the door.' 'What would I come in for?' Molly would ask with a great air of surprise. ''Pon my soul,' Charlie would say admiringly, 'you're most captivating.' 'Captivating?' Molly would shriek. 'Listen to him, you sweet God! There's capers for you!' 'You're like a rose,' Charlie would say and then give one wild bound out of the bed that landed him within a few feet of her, while Molly, shrieking with laughter, banged the door behind her.

It was undoubtedly the slander on his manhood which interested Charlie in Molly, though it would be going too far to say that he had no other object than to disprove it. He liked Molly, and more than ever with Polly and his mother round the house she seemed like a rose. Sometimes when they were out he followed her upstairs and skirmished with her. She let on to be very shocked. 'Sweet Jesus!' she cried, 'What would I do if one of them walked in on me? And all the holy pictures!' She flashed a wondering look at all the coloured pictures, the statues, and the Lourdes clock. 'Isn't it true for me?' she cried. 'A wonder you wouldn't have a bit of shame in you!'

'As a matter of fact,' said Charlie gravely, 'that's the idea. You knew I was starting a religious order of my own here, didn't you?'

'A religious order?' echoed Molly. 'I did not.'

'Oh, yes, yes,' said Charlie importantly. 'I'm only waiting on the authority from Rome.'

'What sort of religious order?' asked Molly suspiciously – she was not too bright in the head and, as she said herself, with that thundering blackguard, Charlie Cashman, you'd never know where you were.

'An order of Christian married couples,' replied Charlie. 'The old sort of marriage is a washout. Purity is what we're going in for.'

'Purity?' shrieked Molly in a gale of laughter. 'And you in it!'

Secretly she was delighted to see Charlie among all 'them old holy ones', as she called them, showing such spunk, and couldn't bear to deprive him of his little pleasure. She didn't deprive him of it long.

And then one autumn evening she whispered to him that she was going to have a baby. She wept and said her old fellow would have her sacred life, which was likely enough, seeing that her father preferred to correct his large family with a razor. Charlie shed a few tears as well and told her not to mind her old

fellow; while he had a pound in the bank he'd never see her
short of anything. He meant it too, because he was a warm-
hearted man and had always kept a soft spot for Molly. But
what really moved and thrilled him was that in spite of everybody he was at last going to be a father. His doubts about his
manhood were set at rest. In the dusk he went up to Johnny
Desmond's overflowing with delight and good humour. He
cracked half a dozen jokes at Morgan in quick succession and
made them all wonder what he had up his sleeve. From this
out they could pass what dirty remarks they liked, but these
would be nothing compared with his secret laugh at them.
It didn't matter if it took twenty years before they knew. He
was in the wildest spirits, drinking and joking and making up
rhymes.

Next morning, coming on to dawn, he woke with a very bad
taste in his mouth. He glanced round and there, in the light of
the colza-oil lamp that burned before the statue of the Sacred
Heart, saw Polly beside him in the bed. She looked determined
even in sleep. The Lourdes clock, which was suffering from
hallucinations and imagining it was an alarm clock, was kicking up merry hell on the mantelpiece. He knew it was really
playing 'The bell of the Angelus calleth to pray', which is a
nice, soothing, poetic thought, but what it said in his mind
was: 'You're caught, Charlie Cashman, you can't get away.'
He realized that, instead of escaping, he had only wedged himself more firmly in the trap, that if ever the truth about Molly
became known, Polly would leave him, the Donegans would
hound him down, Father Ring would denounce him from the
altar, and his little business would go to pot. And in spite of it
all he would not be able to leave the business to his son. 'You're
caught, Charlie Cashman, you can't get away,' sang the clock
with a sort of childish malice.

The skill with which he manoeuvred Molly out of the house
would have done credit to an international statesman. He
found her lodgings in Asragh and put some money to her name
in the bank without anyone being the wiser. But in crises it is
never the difficulties you can calculate on that really upset you.
How could anyone have guessed that Molly, without a job to

do, would find her time a burden and spend hours in the Redemptorist church? After a couple of months Charlie started to receive the most alarming letters. Molly talked of telling Polly, of telling her father, of spending the rest of her days in a home doing penance. Charlie was getting thoroughly fed up with religion. When he saw her one night in a back street in Asragh – the only place where they could meet in comparative safety – he was shocked at the change in her. She was plumper and better-looking but her eyes were shadowy and her voice had dropped to a sort of whine.

'Oh, Charlie,' she sighed with a lingering, come-to-Christ air, 'what luck or grace could we have and the life of sin and deception we're leading?'

'A lot of deception and damn little sin,' Charlie said bitterly. 'What the hell do you want?'

'Oh, Charlie, I want you to put an end to the deception as well as the sin. Be said by me and confess it to your wife.'

'What a thing I'd do!' Charlie said, scowling and stamping. 'Do you know what she'd do?'

'What would any woman do and she finding you truly repentant?' asked Molly ecstatically.

'She'd take bloody good care I had cause,' said Charlie.

He persuaded her out of that particular mood but all the same he wasn't sure of her. It was a nerve-racking business. In the evenings after his supper he lit his pipe and took his usual prowl to the door but he couldn't bring himself to leave the house. Nora Lawlor might drop in while he was away and tell the whole thing to Polly. He had a trick of making up little rhymes to amuse himself, and one that he made at this time ran:

> Brass, boys, brass, and not only buttons,
> The older we gets, the more we toughens.

Charlie didn't toughen at all, unfortunately.

'Wisha, wouldn't you go for a little stroll?' Polly would ask considerately.

'Ah, I don't feel like it,' Charlie would say with a sigh.

'Oh, Law!' she would cry in gentle surprise. 'Isn't that a great change for you, Charlie?'

Once or twice he nearly snapped at her and asked whose fault it was. Sometimes he went to the house door and stood there for a full half-hour with his shoulder against the jamb, drinking in the misery of the view in the winter dusk: the one mean Main Street where everyone knew him and no one wished him well. It was all very fine for Romeo, but Romeo hadn't to live in an Irish country town. Each morning he prowled about in wait for Christy Flynn, the postman, to intercept any anonymous letter there might be for Polly. As he didn't know which of them were anonymous, he intercepted them all.

Then one morning the blow fell. It was a solicitor's letter. He left the shop in charge of Polly and went down to Curwen Street to see his own solicitor, Timsy Harrington. Curwen Street is a nice quiet Georgian street, rosy and warm even on a winter's day, and signs on it; the cheapest call you could pay there would cost you a pound. Charlie knew his call would cost him more than that, but he smoked his pipe and tried to put a brave face on it, as though he thought actions for seduction the best sport in the world. That didn't go down with Timsy Harrington, though.

'Mr Cashman,' he said in his shrill, scolding, old woman's voice, 'I'm surprised at you. I'm astonished at you. An educated man like you! You had the whole country to choose from and no one would do you but a daughter of Jim O'Regan, that stopped in bed with his son for eight months, hoping to get a couple of pounds out of the insurance company.'

Charlie went back along the Main Street feeling as though he were bleeding from twenty gashes. He swore that if ever he got out of this scrape he'd live a celibate for the rest of his days. People said the woman always paid, but the particular occasion when she did was apparently forgotten. Outside the shop he was accosted by an old countryman with a long innocent face.

'Good morrow, Charlie,' he said confidentially, giving Charlie a glimpse of a plug in the palm of his hand. 'I wonder would you have the comrade of this?'

'I'll try, Tom,' said Charlie with a sigh, taking it from him and turning it over in his hand. 'Leave me this and I'll see what I can do. I'm very busy at the moment.'

He opened the shop door, and knew at once that there was trouble in the wind. There was no one in the shop. He stood at the door with his ear cocked. He heard Polly moving with stallion strides about the bedroom and his heart misgave him. He knew well the Lawlor one had profited by his absence. Already the solicitor's letter was public property. He went up the stairs and opened the bedroom door a few inches. Polly was throwing clothes, shoes, and statues all together in a couple of suitcases with positive frenzy. Charlie pushed in the door a little farther, looked at the suitcases, then at her, and finally managed to work up what he thought of as an insinuating smile.

'What's up, little girl?' he asked with a decent show of innocent gaiety.

He saw from her look that this particular line was a complete washout, so he entered cautiously, closing the door behind him for fear of being overheard from the shop.

'Aren't I in trouble enough?' he asked bitterly. 'Do you know what the O'Regans want out of me?'

'Oh,' cried Polly with the air of a tragedy queen, 'if there was a man among them he'd shoot you!'

'Two hundred pounds!' hissed Charlie, his high hairy cheekbones twitching. 'Isn't that a nice how-d'ye-do?'

'Oh,' she cried distractedly, 'you're worse than the wild beasts. The wild beasts have some modesty but you have none. It was my own fault. Nora Lawlor warned me.'

'Nora Lawlor will be the ruination of you,' Charlie said severely. 'She was in here again this morning – you needn't tell me. I can see the signs of her.'

'Don't attempt to criticize her to me!' stormed Polly. 'Get out of my sight or I won't be responsible. The servant!'

'Whisht, woman, whisht, whisht, whisht!' hissed Charlie, dancing in a fury of apprehension. 'You'll be heard from the shop.'

'Oh, I'll take care to be heard,' said Polly, giving her rich voice full play. 'I'll let them know the sort of man they're dealing with. I'll soho you well.'

'So this is married life!' muttered Charlie in a wounded voice, turning away. Then he paused and looked at her over his shoulder as if he couldn't believe it. 'Merciful God,' he said, 'what sort of woman are you at all? How well I didn't go on like this about the schoolmaster!'

'What schoolmaster?' Polly asked in bewilderment, her whole face taking on a ravaged air.

'Carmody,' said Charlie reproachfully. 'You thought it was my fault and I thought it was yours – what more was in it? We both acted with a good purpose. Surely to God,' he added anxiously, 'you don't think I did it for pleasure?'

'Oh,' she cried, beside herself, 'wait till I tell Father Ring! Wait till he knows the sort of comparisons you're making! With a good purpose! Oh, you blasphemer! How the earth doesn't open and swallow you!'

She pushed him out and slammed the door behind him. Charlie stood on the landing and gave a brokenhearted sigh. 'So this is married life!' he repeated despairingly. He returned to the shop and stood far back at the rear, leaning against the stovepipe. It was a sunny morning and the sunlight streamed through the windows and glinted on the bright buckets hanging outside the door. He saw Nora Lawlor, wearing a scarlet coat, come out of the butcher's and give a furtive glance across the street. If he had had a gun with him he would have shot her dead.

He heard Polly come downstairs and open the hall door. Slowly and on tiptoe he went to the door of the shop, leaned his shoulder against the jamb and looked up the street after Nora. He saw her red coat disappear round the corner by the chapel. The old farmer who was waiting outside the post office thought that Charlie was hailing him, but Charlie frowned and shook his head. From the hall he heard Polly address a small boy in that clear voice of hers which he knew could be heard all along the street.

'Dinny,' she said, 'I want you to run down to Hennessey's and ask them to send up a car.'

Charlie was so overcome that he retreated to the back of the shop again. Polly was leaving him. It would be all round the town in five minutes. Yet he knew he wasn't a bad man; there were plenty worse and their wives didn't leave them. For one wild moment he thought of making a last appeal to her love, but one glance into the hall at Polly sitting bolt-upright in her blue serge costume, her cases beside her and her gloves and prayer-book on the hallstand, and he knew that love wasn't even in the running. He went to the shop door and beckoned to another small boy.

'I want you to find Father Ring and bring him here quick,' he whispered fiercely, pressing a coin into the child's palm. 'Mr Cashman sent you, say. And tell him hurry!'

'Is it someone sick, Mr Cashman?' asked the little boy eagerly.

'Yes,' hissed Charlie. 'Dying. Hurry now!'

After that he paced up and down the shop like a caged tiger till he saw Father Ring rounding the corner by the chapel. He went up to meet him.

'What is it at all, Charlie?' the priest asked anxiously. 'Is it the mother?'

'No, Father,' Charlie said desperately, seeing the twitching of curtains in top rooms. 'I only wish to God it was,' he ground out in a frenzy.

'Is it as bad as that, Charlie?' Father Ring asked in concern as they entered the shop.

'Ah, I'm in great trouble, Father,' Charlie said, tossing his head like a wounded animal. Then he fixed his gaze on a spot of light at the back of the shop and addressed himself to it. 'I don't know did you hear any stories about me,' he inquired guardedly.

'Stories, Charlie?' exclaimed Father Ring, who, being a Kerryman, could fight a better delaying-action than Charlie himself. 'What sort of stories?'

'Well, now, Father, not the sort you'd like to hear,' replied Charlie with what for him was almost candour.

'Well, now you mention it, Charlie,' said Father Ring with equal frankness, 'I fancy I did hear something ... Not, of course, that I believed it,' he added hastily, for fear he might be committing himself too far.

'I'm sorry to say you can, Father,' said Charlie, bowing his head and joining his hands before him as he did at Mass on Sunday.

'Oh, my, my, Charlie,' said Father Ring, giving him a look out of the corner of his eye, 'that's bad.'

Charlie looked at the floor and nodded glumly a couple of times to show he shared the priest's view of it.

'And tell me, Charlie,' whispered Father Ring, pivoting on his umbrella as he leaned closer, 'what way did herself take it?'

'Badly, Father,' replied Charlie severely. 'Very badly. I must say I'm disappointed in Polly.'

This time it was he who looked out of the corner of his eye and somehow it struck him that Father Ring was not as shocked-looking as he might have been.

'I'd expect that, mind you,' Father Ring said thoughtfully.

'By God, he isn't shocked!' thought Charlie. There was something that almost resembled fellow-feeling in his air.

'But heavens above, Father,' Charlie said explosively, 'the woman is out of her mind. And as for that Lawlor girl, I don't know what to say to her.' Father Ring nodded again, as though to say that he didn't know either. 'Of course, she's a good-living girl and all the rest of it,' Charlie went on cantankerously, 'but girls with no experience of life have no business interfering between married couples. It was bad enough without her – I needn't tell you that. And there she is now,' he added, cocking his thumb in the direction of the hall, 'with her bags packed and after ordering a car up from Hennessey's. Sure that's never right.'

'Well, now, Charlie,' Father Ring whispered consolingly, 'women are contrairy; they are contrairy, there's no denying that. I'll have a word with her myself.'

He opened the house door gently, peeped in, and then went into the hall on tiptoe, as if he were entering a room where someone was asleep. Charlie held the door slightly open behind him to hear what went on. Unfortunately, the sight of the priest going in had given the old farmer the notion of business as usual. Charlie looked round and saw his long mournful face in the doorway.

'Charlie,' he began, 'if I'm not disturbing you—'

Charlie, raising his clenched fists in the air, did a silent war-dance. The old farmer staggered back, cut to the heart, and then sat on the sill of the window with his stick between his legs. When another farmer came by the old man began to tell him his troubles with long, accusing glances back at Charlie, who was glued to the door with an agonized look on his face.

'My poor child!' he heard Father Ring say in a shocked whisper. 'You were in the wars. I can see you were.'

'Well, I'm going home now, Father,' Polly replied listlessly.

'Sure, where better could you go?' exclaimed Father Ring as if trying to disabuse her of any idea she might have of staying on. ' 'Tis that husband of yours, I suppose? 'Tis to be sure. I need hardly ask.'

'I'd rather not talk about it, Father,' Polly said politely but firmly. 'I dare say you'll hear all about it soon enough.'

'I dare say I will,' he agreed. 'People in this town don't seem to have much better to do. 'Pon my word, I believe I saw a few curtains stirring on my way down. You'll have an audience.'

'I never minded much what they saw,' said Polly wearily.

'Sure, you never had anything to conceal,' said Father Ring, overwhelming her with agreement, as his way was. 'I suppose you remember the case of that little girl from Parnell Street a few weeks ago?'

'No, Father, I'm afraid I don't,' replied Polly without interest.

'Sure, you couldn't be bothered. Ah, 'twas a sad business, though. Married at ten and the baby born at onc.'

'Oh, my, Father,' said Polly politely, 'wasn't that very quick?'

'Well, now you mention it, Polly, it was. But that wasn't what I was going to say. The poor child came home at four in the morning to avoid attracting attention, and would you believe me, Polly, not a soul in Parnell Street went to bed that night! Sure, that's never natural! I say that's not natural. Where's that blackguard of a husband of yours till I give him a bit of my mind? Charlie Cashman! Charlie Cashman! Where are you, you scoundrel?'

'I'm here, Father,' said Charlie meekly, taking two steps forward till he stood between the crimson curtains with a blaze of silver from the fanlight falling on his bowed head.

'Aren't you ashamed of yourself?' shouted the priest, raising the umbrella to him.

'I am, Father, I am, I am,' replied Charlie in a broken voice without looking up.

'Oh, that's only all old connoisseuring, Father,' Polly cried distractedly, jumping to her feet and grabbing gloves and prayer-book. 'No one knows what I went through with that man.' She opened the hall door; the hall was flooded with silver light, and she turned to them, drawing a deep breath through her nose, as beautiful and menacing as a sibyl. 'I'm going home to my father now,' she continued in a firm voice. 'I left my keys on the dressing-table and you can give Hennessey's boy the bags.'

'Polly,' Father Ring said sternly, leaning on his umbrella, 'what way is this for a Child of Mary to behave?'

'As, 'tis all very fine for you to talk, Father,' Polly cried scoldingly. 'You don't have to live with him. I'd sooner live with a wild beast than with that man,' she added dramatically.

'Polly,' Father Ring said mildly, 'what you do in your own house is your business. What you do in the public view is mine. Polly, you're in the public view.'

For the first time in Charlie's life he found himself admiring Father Ring. There was a clash and a grating of wills like the bending of steel girders, and suddenly Polly's girders buckled. She came in and closed the door. 'Now, Polly,' Father Ring said affectionately, 'inside that door I don't want to interfere between ye, good or bad. Make what arrangements you like. Live with him or don't live with him; sleep in the loft or sleep in the stable, but don't let me have any more scandal like we had this morning.'

'I wouldn't be safe from him in the stable,' Polly said rebelliously. She felt that for the first time in her life she had been met and mastered by a man, and it rankled. There was more than a joke in Charlie's suggestion that it was Father Ring she should have married. If only she could have gone to bed with him then and there she would probably have risen a normal woman. But deprived of this consolation she was ready to turn nasty, and Father Ring saw it. Charlie only noticed the false-hood about himself.

'You wouldn't be what?' he cried indignantly. 'When did I ever raise a finger or say a cross word to you?'

'Now, Charlie, now!' Father Ring said shortly, raising his hand for silence. 'And woman alive,' he asked good-humoured-ly, 'can't you bolt your door?'

'How can I,' stormed Polly, as sulky as a spoiled child, 'when there's no bolt on it?'

'That's easily remedied.'

'Then tell him send out for a carpenter and have it done now,' she said vindictively.

'Send out for a what?' shouted Charlie, cocking his head as if he couldn't believe what he heard. 'Is it mad you are? What a thing I'd do!'

'Very well,' she said, opening the hall door again. 'I'll go home to my father.'

'Hold on now, hold on!' Charlie cried frantically, dragging her back and closing the door behind her. 'I'll do it myself.'

'Then do it now!' she cried.

'Do what she says, Charlie,' the priest said quietly. He saw that the danger wasn't over yet. Charlie gave her a murderous glare and went out to the shop. A crowd had gathered outside on the pavement, discussing the wrongs of the poor farmer, who was an object of the most intense sympathy. Charlie re-turned with a brass bolt, a screwdriver, and a couple of screws.

'Show me that bolt!' said Polly menacingly. The devil was up in her now. The priest might have bested her but she still saw a way of getting her own back. Charlie knew that next day she and Nora Lawlor would be splitting their sides over it; women were like that, and he vowed a holy war against the whole boiling of them to the day of his death. 'I'm going home to my father's,' she said, clamping her long lips. 'That bolt is too light.'

'Get a heavier one, Charlie,' Father Ring said quietly. 'Don't argue, there's a good man!'

Argument was about the last thing in Charlie's mind at that moment. Murder would have been nearer the mark. He flung the bolt at Polly's feet but she didn't even glance at him. When he returned to the shop the crowd was surging round the door.

'Bad luck and end to ye!' he snarled, taking out his spleen on them. 'Have ye no business of yeer own to mind without nosing round here?'

'Mr Cashman,' said a young man whom Charlie recognized as the old farmer's son, 'you have a plug belonging to my father.'

'Then take it and to hell with ye!' snarled Charlie, taking the plug from his pocket and throwing it into the midst of them.

'Oh, begor, we won't trouble you much from this day forth,' the young man said fierily. 'Nor more along with us.'

That was the trouble in a quarrel with a countryman. There always were more along with him. Charlie, aware that he might have seriously injured his business, returned to the hall with an iron bolt. 'That's a stable bolt,' he said, addressing no one in particular.

'Put it on,' said Polly.

Charlie went upstairs. Father Ring followed him. The priest stood in awe, looking at all the holy pictures. Then he held the bolt while Charlie used the screwdriver. Charlie was so mad that he used it anyhow.

'You're putting that screw in crooked, Charlie,' said the priest. 'Wait now till I put on my specs and I'll do it for you.'

'Let her go! Let her go!' said Charlie on the point of a breakdown. 'It doesn't matter to me whether she goes or stays. I'm nothing only a laughing-stock.'

'Now, Charlie, Charlie,' said the priest good-naturedly, 'you have your little business to mind.'

'For my nephews to walk into,' said Charlie bitterly.

'God spoke first, Charlie,' the priest said gravely. 'You're a young man yet. Begor,' he added, giving Charlie a quizzical look over the specs, 'I did a few queer jobs in my time but this is the queerest yet.' He saw that Charlie was in no state to appreciate the humour of it, and gave him a professional look through the spectacles. 'Ah, well, Charlie,' he said, 'we all have our burdens. You have only one, but I have a dozen, not to mention the nuns, and they reckon two on a count.'

As they came down the stairs Charlie's mother appeared out of the kitchen as if from nowhere, drying her hands in her apron; a little bundle of rags, bones and malice, with a few wisps of white hair blowing about her.

'Aha,' she cackled as if she were speaking to herself, 'I hear the Holy Door is shut for the next seven years.'

8

But, as she was so fond of saying herself, 'God spoke first.' It seemed as if Polly never had another day's luck. She fell into a slow decline and made herself worse instead of better by drinking the stuff Mrs Cashman brought her from the Wise Woman, and by changing from the Nine Fridays to the Nine Tuesdays and from the Nine Tuesdays to the Nine Mondays on the advice of Nora Lawlor, who had tried them all.

A scandal of that sort is never good for a man's business. The Donegans and their friends paid their accounts and went elsewhere. The shop began to go down and Charlie went with it. He paid less attention to his appearance, served the counter unshaven and without collar and tie; grew steadily shabbier and more irritable and neglected-looking. He spent most of his evenings in Johnny Desmond's, but even there people fought shy of him. The professional men and civil servants treated him as a sort of town character, a humorous, unreliable fellow without much balance. To Charlie, who felt they were only cashing in on the sacrifices of men like himself, this was the bitterest blow, and in his anxiety to keep his end up before them he boasted, quarrelled, and generally played the fool.

But the funny thing was that from the time she fell ill Polly herself softened towards him. Her family were the first to notice it. Like everything else in Polly it went to extremes, and indeed it occurred to her mother that if the Almighty God in His infinite mercy didn't release her soon, she'd have no religion left.

'I don't know is he much worse than anyone else,' she said

broodingly. 'I had some very queer temptations myself that no one knew about. Father Ring said once that I was very unforgiving. I think now he was right. Our family were always vindictive.'

After that she began to complain about being nervous alone and Mrs Cashman offered to sleep with her.

'Oh, I could never bear another woman in the room with me,' Polly said impatiently. 'What I want is a man. I think I'll ask Charlie to make it up.'

'Is it that fellow?' cried Charlie's mother, aghast. 'That scut – that – I have no words for him. Oh, my! A man that would shame his poor wife the way that ruffian did!'

'Ah, the way ye talk one'd think he never stopped,' Polly said fractiously. 'Ye have as much old goings-on about one five minutes!'

At this Mrs Cashman decided she was going soft in the head. When a married woman begins to reckon her husband's infidelities in terms of hours and minutes she is in a bad state. Polly asked Charlie meekly enough to come back and keep her company. Charlie would have been as well pleased to stay as he was, where he could come and go as he liked, but he saw it was some sort of change before death.

It was cold comfort for Polly. Too much mischief had been made between them for Charlie to feel about her as a man should feel for his wife. They would lie awake in the grey, flickering light of the colza-oil lamp, with all the holy pictures round them and the Lourdes clock on the mantelpiece ticking away whenever it remembered it and making wild dashes to catch up on lost time, and Charlie's thoughts would wander and he would think that if Polly were once out of the way he would have another chance of a woman who would fling herself into his arms without asking Father Ring's permission, like the Yeoman Captain's Daughter in the old song:

> *A thousand pounds I'll give thee*
> *And fly from home with thee;*
> *I'll dress myself in man's attire*
> *And fight for Liberty.*

Charlie was a romantic, and he couldn't get over his boyish notion that there must be women like the Captain's Daughter, if only you could meet them. And while he was making violent love to her, Polly, lying beside him, thought of how her poor bare bones would soon be scattered on the stony little patch above Kilmurray while another woman would be lying in her bed. It made her very bitter.

'I suppose you're only waiting till the sod is over me?' she said one night in a low voice when Charlie was just fancying that she must have dropped off.

'What's that?' he asked in astonishment and exasperation, looking at her with one arm under her head, staring into the shadows.

'You're only waiting till I'm well rotten to get another woman in my place,' she went on accusingly.

'What a thing I'd think of!' Charlie snapped, as cross as a man jolted out of his sleep, for her words had caught the skirts of the Captain's Daughter as she slipped out of the room, and Charlie felt it was shameful for him in his health and strength to be contriving like that against a sick woman.

'Nothing matters to you now only to best John Joe and have a son that'll come in for the shop,' said Polly with the terrible insight of the last loneliness. 'Only for the shop you might have some nature for me.'

'And when the hell had I anything but nature for you?' he shouted indignantly, sitting up. 'What do you think I married you for? Money?'

'If you had any nature for me you wouldn't disrespect me,' Polly went on stubbornly, clinging to her grievance.

'And what about you?' said Charlie. 'You had to think I was some old devil on the pictures before you could put up with me. There's nature for you!'

'I did it with a good object,' said Polly.

'Good object!' snorted Charlie. He almost told her that Juliet and the Captain's Daughter didn't do it with a good object or any object at all only getting the man they wanted, but he knew she wouldn't understand. Polly lay for a long time drawing deep breaths through her nose.

'Don't think or imagine I'll rest quiet and see you married to another woman,' she added in a very determined voice. 'You may think you'll be rid of me but I'll make full sure you won't. All our family would go to hell's gates to be revenged.'

'Christ Almighty,' snarled Charlie, giving one wild leap out of the bed, 'leave me out of this! This is my thanks for coming back here! Leave me out!'

'Mind what I say now,' said Polly in an awe-inspiring voice, pointing a bony arm at him from the shadows. She knew she had him on a sore spot. Herself or Mrs Cashman would have made no more fuss about meeting a ghost than about meeting the postman, but Charlie had enough of the rationalist in him to be terrified. His mother had brought him up on them. 'Our family was ever full of ghosts,' she added solemnly. 'You won't have much comfort with her.'

'My trousers!' cried Charlie, beside himself with rage and terror. 'Where the hell is my trousers?'

'I'm giving you fair warning,' Polly cried in bloodcurdling tones as he poked his way out of the room in his nightshirt. 'I'll soho ye well, the pair of ye!'

9

She died very peacefully one evening when no one was in the room but old Mrs Cashman. Even in death she made trouble for Charlie. Her last wish was to be buried in Closty, the Donegan graveyard. It wasn't that she bore any malice to Charlie, but the thought of the two wives in one grave upset her. She said it wouldn't be nice, and Nora agreed with her. Of course, when it got out it made things worse for Charlie, for it suggested that, at the very least, he had some hand in her death.

Nora felt rather like that too, but then a strange thing happened. She was coming down from the bedroom when she heard a noise from the shop. The door was closed, all but an inch or two, but Nora was of a very inquisitive disposition. She pushed it in. The shop was dark, several of the outside shutters being up, but in the dim light she saw the figure of a man and realized that the noise she had heard was weeping. It gave her a shock, for it had never once occurred to her that Charlie was that sort of man. She was a warm-hearted girl. She went up and touched his arm.

'I'm sorry, Charlie,' she said timidly.

'I know that, Nora,' he muttered without looking round. 'I know you are.'

'She'll be a terrible loss,' she added, more from want of something to say than the feeling that she was speaking the truth.

'Ah, she was unfortunate, Nora,' Charlie said with a sob. 'She was a fine woman, a lovely woman. I don't know what bad luck was on us.'

'What better luck could ye have and the poor orphan cheated?' cried a harsh, inexpressive voice from the hall. Nora started. Mrs Cashman was standing in the doorway with her hands on her hips. Her voice and appearance were like those of an apparition, and for the first time Nora wondered if there wasn't something in Polly's fancy that she was really a witch. 'She's better off, Nora girl.'

'I suppose so,' Nora agreed doubtfully, resenting her intrusion just at the moment when Charlie was ready for confidences. People with tears in their eyes will tell you things they'd never tell you at other times.

'She was a good girl and a just girl and she loved her God,' hissed Mrs Cashman, aiming every word at Charlie under Nora's guard. 'It would be a bad man that would go against her dying wishes.'

'Who talked of going against them?' snarled Charlie with the savagery of a goaded beast, and lunging past them went out and banged the hall door behind him.

'Poor Charlie is very upset,' said Nora.

'Upset?' cackled Mrs Cashman. 'How upset he is! She's not in her grave yet, and already he's planning who he'll get instead of her. That's how upset he is! But he's not done with me yet, the blackguard!'

For the first time it occurred to Nora that perhaps Charlie had been misjudged – if men could ever be misjudged. From all accounts of what they did to poor women when they had them stripped, they could not, but something about Mrs Cashman made her suspicious.

She went to the funeral in Mrs Cashman's carriage. The moment she got out of it at the graveyard she knew there was trouble in store. The Donegans were there, a half-dozen different families, and on their own ground they had taken complete command. Charlie was only an outsider. He stood by the hearse with his hands crossed before him, holding his hat, and a look of desperation on his dark face. Others besides herself had noticed the signs, and a group of men was standing in a semicircle a hundred yards down the road, where they wouldn't get involved. Her father was between them and the hearse, but sufficiently far away to keep out of it as well. He was scowling, his lips pouted, his eyes were half shut while he noticed everything that went on.

The procession into the graveyard would be the signal. Charlie would be shouldered away from the cemetery gate, and he knew it, and knew he was no match for half a dozen men younger than himself. He'd fight, of course; everyone who knew Charlie knew that, but he could be very quickly dragged down the lane and no one much the wiser. Just at the moment when the coffin was eased out of the hearse and four Donegans got under it Nora left Mrs Cashman's side and stood by Charlie.

It was exactly as though she had blown a policeman's whistle. Her father raised his head and beckoned to the semicircle of men behind and then, pulling the lapels of his coat together, placed himself at the other side of her. One by one half a dozen middle-aged men came up and joined Charlie's party. They were all old Volunteers and could not stand aside and let their Commandant and Vice-Commandant be hustled about by the seed of land-grabbers and policemen. Not a word was spoken, not a cross look exchanged, but everyone knew that sides had been taken and that Charlie could now enter the graveyard unmolested. As he and Nora emerged at the grave Father Ring looked up at them from under his bushy brows. He had missed none of the drama. There was very little that foxy little man missed.

'Thanks, Nora, thanks,' said Charlie in a low voice as the service ended. 'You were always a good friend.'

Even Nora at her most complacent wouldn't have described herself as a friend of Charlie's, but the fact that he had understood what she had done proved him to have better feelings than she had given him credit for. She was embarrassed by the feelings she had roused. The old Volunteers all came up and shook her formally by the hand. Her father was the most surprising of all. He stood aside sniffing, with tears in his eyes, too overcome even to tell her what he felt.

After that, everyone noticed the change in Charlie. His clothes were brushed, his boots were polished, his face was shaved, and no matter what hour of the morning you went in he had collar and tie on. He spent more time in the shop and less in Johnny Desmond's. He even gave up going to Johnny's altogether. That could only mean that he was looking for someone to take Polly's place. But who would have him? A respectable woman would be lowering herself. The general impression was that he'd marry Molly O'Regan, and Nora supposed that this would only be right, but somehow she couldn't help feeling it would be a pity. Mrs Cashman, who saw all her beautiful plans for her grandchildren go up in smoke, felt the same. For the first time Nora included Charlie in her prayers, and asked the Holy Ghost to help him in making the right choice.

One night a few weeks later on her way back from the church she looked in on him. She was astonished at Mrs Cashman's sourness.

'You'll have a cup of tea?' said Charlie.

'I won't Charlie, honest,' she said hastily, alarmed at the puss the old woman had on her. 'I'm rushing home.'

'I'll see you home,' he said at once, giving himself a glance in the mirror.

'If you're back before me, the key will be in the window,' Mrs Cashman said sourly.

'You're not going out again?' he asked.

'I'm not going to stop in this house alone,' she bawled.

'Really, Charlie, there's no reason for you to come,' said Nora in distress.

'Nonsense!' he snapped crossly. 'Herself and her ghosts!'

It was a moonlit night and the street was split with silver light. The abbey tower was silhouetted against it, and the light broke through the deeply splayed chancel lancets, making deep shadows among the foundered tombstones.

'I only came to know how you were getting on,' she said.

'Ah, I'm all right,' said Charlie. 'Only a bit lonesome, of course.'

'Ah,' she said with a half-smile, 'I suppose you won't be long that way.'

She could have dropped dead with shame as soon as she had said it. Nora was never one to make any bones about her inquisitiveness, but this sounded positively vulgar. It wasn't in line at all with her behaviour at the funeral. Charlie didn't seem to notice. He gave her a long look through screwed-up eyes, and then crossed the road to lean his back against the bridge.

'Tell me, Nora,' he asked, folding his arms and looking keenly at her from under the peak of his cap, 'what would you do in my position?'

'Oh, I don't know, Charlie,' she replied in alarm, wondering how she could extricate herself from the consequences of her own curiosity. 'What's to prevent you?'

'You know the sort of things Polly said?' he said with a sigh.

'I don't think I'd mind that at all,' she replied. 'After all, Polly was a very sick woman.'

'She was,' agreed Charlie. 'Do you think 'twould be right to go against her wishes like that?'

'Well, of course, that would depend, Charlie,' said Nora with sudden gravity, for like many of her race she combined a strong grasp of the truths of religion with a hazy notion of the facts of life.

'You mean on whether 'twas done with a good object or not?' Charlie asked keenly. All he had learned from years with Polly was the importance of doing things with a good object.

'And whether the wishes were reasonable or not,' she added, surprised to find him so well versed in religious matters.

'And you don't think they were?'

'I wouldn't say so. Father Ring could tell you that better than I could.'

'I dare say, I dare say. Tell me, Nora, do you believe in things like that?'

'Like what, Charlie?' she asked in surprise.

'Ghosts, and things of that sort,' he said with a nervous glance in the direction of the abbey, whose slender tapering tower soared from the rubbish-tip of ruined gables, with its tall irregular battlements that looked like cockades in the moonlight.

'We're taught to believe in them,' she replied with a little shudder.

'I know we are,' sighed Charlie. 'But you never saw one yourself?'

'I didn't.'

'Nor I.'

They resumed their walk home. Nora saw now what was fretting him. Polly had said she'd haunt him and Polly was a woman of her word. Anything she had ever said she'd do she had done, and there was no saying that as a pure spirit she'd have changed much. Charlie himself had lost a lot of the cocksure rationalism of his fighting days. He had lived so long with women that he was becoming almost as credulous as they. He was reckoning up his chances in case Polly's ghost got out of hand. Nora couldn't give him much comfort, for her own belief in ghosts was determined by the time of day, and at ten o'clock of a moonlight night it was always particularly strong.

When they parted she blamed herself a lot. It was most unmaidenly of her first to call at all and, secondly, to ask point blank what his intentions were, for that was what it amounted to, and for a terrible few minutes she had dreaded that he might think it mattered to her. Of course it didn't, except for his own sake, because though she had begun to like him better, she knew there was no possibility of a Child of Mary like herself marrying him – even if Polly had been an unobtrusive ghost.

She would have been surprised and upset to know that her

views were not shared by others. When Charlie got home he stood in the hall in surprise. There was something queer about the house. The hall was in darkness; there was light in the kitchen but it was very feeble. With all the talk of ghosts it upset him. 'Are you there, Mother?' he called nervously, but there was no reply, only the echo of his own voice. He went to the kitchen door and his heart almost stopped beating. The fire was out, the greater part of the room in shadow, but two candles in two brass candlesticks were burning on the mantelpiece, and between them, smiling down at him, a large, silver-framed photo of Polly.

Next moment, seeing how he was being baited, he went mad with rage. His mother, the picture of aged innocence, was kneeling by her bed when he went in, and she looked round at him in surprise.

'Was it you left that in the kitchen?' he shouted.

'What is it?' she asked in mock ignorance, rising and screwing up her eyes as she reached for the picture. 'Oh, isn't it pretty?' she asked. 'I found it today in one of her drawers.'

'Put it back where you found it,' he stormed.

'Oye, why?' she asked with a pretence of concern, 'Wouldn't anyone like it – his poor, dead wife? Unless he'd have something on his conscience.'

'Never mind my conscience,' shouted Charlie. 'Fitter for you to look after your own.'

'Aha,' she bawled triumphantly, throwing off the mask, 'my conscience have nothing to trouble it.'

'You have it too well seasoned.'

'And don't think but she sees it all, wherever she is,' the old woman cried, raising her skinny paw in the direction in which Polly might be supposed to exist. 'Take care she wouldn't rise from the grave and haunt you, you and that little whipster you were out gallivanting with!'

'What gallivanting?' snarled Charlie. 'You don't know what you're talking about.'

'Maybe I'm blind!' bawled his mother. 'Walking into the graveyard alongside you, as if she had you caught already! Aha, the sly-boots, the pussycat, with her novenas and her Nine

Fridays! She thinks we don't know what she's up to, but God sees ye, and the dead woman sees ye, and what's more, I see ye. And mark my words, Charlie Cashman, that's the hand that'll never rock a cradle for you!'

10

Two days later Charlie happened to be serving behind the counter when he saw Father Ring busily admiring the goods in the shop window. The priest smiled and nodded, but when Charlie made to come out to him he shook his head warningly. Then he raised one finger and pointed in the direction of the house door. Charlie nodded gloomily. Father Ring made another sign with his thumb to indicate the direction he was going in and Charlie nodded again. He knew Father Ring wanted to talk to him somewhere his mother wouldn't know.

He found Father Ring letting on to be studying the plant life in the river. When Charlie appeared he indicated surprise and pleasure at such an unexpected meeting.

'Whisper, Charlie,' he said at last, putting his left hand on Charlie's shoulder and bending his head discreetly across the other one, 'I had a visit from your mother.'

'My mother?'

'Your mother,' the priest said gravely, studying his face again before making another little excursion over his shoulder. 'She's afraid you're going to get married again,' he whispered in amusement.

'She's easy frightened.'

'That's what I told her. I know you'll keep this to yourself. She seems to think there's some special commandment to stop you. Of course,' added the priest with a shocked air, 'I told her I wouldn't dream of interfering.'

'You did to be sure,' said Charlie watchfully, knowing that this was the one thing in the world that no one could prevent Father Ring from doing.

'You know the girl I mean?'

'I do.'

'A nice girl.'

'A fine girl.'

'And a courageous girl,' said Father Ring. 'Mind you, 'tisn't every girl would do what she did the day of the funeral. Of course,' he admitted, 'she should have been married ten years ago. They get very contrairy.' Then he pounced. 'Tell me, Charlie, you wouldn't be thinking about her, would you? I'm not being inquisitive?'

'You're not, to be sure.'

'Because it struck me that if you were, I might be able to do you a good turn. Of course, she hasn't much experience. You know what I mean?'

'I do, Father,' said Charlie who realized as well as the priest did that it would be no easy job to coax a pious girl like Nora into marriage with a public sinner like himself. But at the same time he was not going to be bounced into anything. He had made a fool of himself once before. 'Well now,' he added with a great air of candour, turning towards the river as though for recollection, 'I'll tell you exactly the way I'm situated, Father. You know the old saying: "Once bitten, twice shy." '

'I do, I do,' said Father Ring, turning in the same direction as if his thought and Charlie's might meet and mingle over the river. Then he started and gave Charlie a look of astonishment. 'Ah, I wouldn't say that, Charlie.'

'Well, maybe I'm putting it a bit strongly, Father.'

'I think so, Charlie, I think you are,' Father Ring said eagerly. 'I'd say she was a different class altogether. More feminine, more clinging – that's under the skin, of course.'

'You might be right, Father,' Charlie said but he stuck to his point all the same. 'But there's one thing you might notice about me,' he went on, looking at the priest out of the corner of his eye. 'You mightn't think it but I'm a highly strung man.'

'You are, you are,' said Father Ring with great anxiety. 'I noticed that myself. I wonder would it be blood pressure, Charlie?'

'I was never the same since the Troubles,' said Charlie. 'But whatever it is, I want something to steady me.'

'You do, you do,' said the priest, trying to follow his drift.

'If I had a family I'd be different.'

'You would,' said Father Ring with a crucified air. 'I can see you're a domesticated sort of man.'

'And,' added Charlie with a wealth of meaning in his tone, 'if the same thing happened me again I might as well throw myself in there.' He pointed at the river, scowling, and then took a deep breath and stepped back from the priest.

'But you don't think it would, Charlie?'

'But you see, Father, I don't know.'

'You don't, you don't, to be sure you don't,' said Father Ring in a glow of understanding. 'I see it now. And, of course, having doubts like that, they might come against you.'

'You put your finger on it.'

'And, of course, if you were to marry the other girl – what's that her name is? – Peggy or Kitty or Joan, you'd have no doubts, and, as well as that, you'd have the little fellow. You could look after him.'

'That's the very thing, Father,' Charlie said savagely. 'That's what has me demented.'

'It has, it has, of course,' said Father Ring, smiling at the sheer simplicity of it. 'Of course, Nora is a nicer girl in every way but a bird in the hand is worth two in the bush. I know exactly how you feel. I'd be the same myself.'

So Charlie returned to the shop, feeling worse than ever. Nora, as Father Ring said, was a nice girl, but a bird in the hand was worth two in the bush and Charlie felt he never really had a bird of any breed; nothing but a few tailfeathers out of Molly before she flew into the bush after the others. And even Father Ring didn't know how badly he felt about Molly's son. He was a warm-hearted man; how else could he feel? Once he had got out the car and driven to the village where the boy had been nursed, watched him come home from school, and then followed him to slip a half-crown into his hand. If only he could bring the little fellow home and see him go to a good school like a Christian, Charlie felt he could put up with a lot from Molly. And he knew that he wouldn't really have to put up with much from her. Under normal circum-stances, there was no moral or intellectual strain that Molly could be subjected to which could not be cured by a hearty smack on the backside.

But then his mind would slip a cog and he would think of the scene outside the graveyard, and Nora, grave and pale, stepping over to his side. 'In comes the Captain's Daughter, the Captain of the Yeos'; 'Romeo, Romeo, wherefore art thou Romeo?' – a couple of lines like those and Charlie would feel himself seventeen again, ready to risk his life for Ireland or anything else that came handy. Whatever misfortune was on him, he knew his mother was right all the time; that he could never be like any other sensible man but would keep on to the day he died, pining for something a bit larger than life.

That night the temptation to go to the pub was almost irresistible. He went as far as the door and then walked on. That was where people went only when their problems had grown too much for them. Instead he went for a lonesome stroll in the country, and as he returned his feet, as if by magic, led him past Nora's door. He passed that too, and then turned back.

'God bless all here,' he said pushing in the door. She was sitting in the dusk and rose to meet him, flushed and eager.

'Come in, Charlie,' she said with real pleasure in her tone. 'You'll have a cup?'

'I'll have a bucket,' said Charlie. 'Since I gave up the booze I have a throat like a lime-kiln.'

'And did you give it up entirely?' she asked with awe.

'Entirely,' said Charlie. 'There's no other way of giving it up.'

'Aren't you great?' she said, but Charlie didn't know whether he was or not. Like all worriers he had at last created a situation for himself that he could really worry about. As she rose to light the gas he stopped her, resting his big paws on her shoulder.

'Sit down,' he said shortly. 'I want to have a word with you.'

Her face grew pale and her big brown eyes took on a wide, unwinking stare as she did what he told her. If Charlie could only have forgotten his own problem for a moment he would have realized that Nora had also hers. Her problem was what she would say if he asked her to marry him.

'I'm in great trouble,' he said.

'Oh, Law!' she exclaimed. 'What is it?'

'I had a talk with Father Ring today.'

'I heard about that.' (There was very little she didn't hear about.)

'He wanted me to get married.'

' 'Tisn't much when you say it quick,' said Nora with rising colour. From Charlie's announcement that he was in trouble she had naturally concluded that Father Ring wanted him to marry Molly and, now that it had come to the point, she didn't really want him to marry Molly. 'I wonder how people can have the audacity to interfere in other people's business like that.'

'Ah, well,' said Charlie, surprised at her warmth, 'he intended it as a kindness.'

'It mightn't turn out to be such a kindness,' said Nora.

'That's the very thing,' said Charlie. 'It might not turn out to be a kindness. That's what I wanted to ask your advice about. You know the way I'm situated. I'm lonely down there with no one only the mother. I know it would probably be the makings of me, but 'tis the risk that has me damned. 'Twould be different if I knew I was going to have a family, someone to come in for the business when I'm gone.'

'You mean the same thing as happened with Polly might happen with her?' Nora exclaimed in surprise.

'I mean I broke my heart once before,' snapped Charlie, 'and I don't want to do it again.'

'But you don't think the same thing would happen again?' she asked with a hypnotized air.

'But I don't know, girl, I don't know,' Charlie cried desperately. 'You might think I'm being unreasonable, but if you went through the same thing with a man that I went through with Polly you'd feel the same. Did Polly ever tell you she thought the mother was putting spells on her?' he added sharply.

'She did.'

'And what do you think of it?'

'I don't know what to think, Charlie,' said Nora, the dusk

having produced its periodical change in her views of the super-natural.

'When I married Polly first,' Charlie went on reflectively, 'she said: "Many a better cake didn't rise." The other night she said: "That's the hand that'll never rock a cradle for you."' He looked at Nora to see if she was impressed, but seeing that Nora in her innocent way applied his mother's prophecy to Molly O'Regan she wasn't as impressed as she might have been if she had known it referred to herself. Charlie felt the scene wasn't going right, but he couldn't see where the error lay. 'What knowledge would a woman like that have?' he asked.

'I couldn't imagine, Charlie,' replied Nora with nothing like the awe he expected.

'So you see the way I am,' he went on after a moment. 'If I don't marry her – always assuming she'd have me, of course,' he interjected tactfully – 'I'm cutting my own throat. If I do marry her and the same thing happens again, I'm cutting her throat as well as my own. What can I do?'

'I'm sure I couldn't advise you, Charlie,' replied Nora steadily, almost as though she was enjoying his troubles, which in a manner of speaking – seeing that her premises were wrong – she was. 'What do you think yourself?'

Charlie didn't quite know what to think. He had come there expecting at least as much sympathy and understanding as he had received from Father Ring. He had felt that even a few tears and kisses wouldn't be out of place.

'If she was a different sort of girl,' he said with an infinity of caution, 'I'd say to her what I said to Father Ring and ask her to come to Dublin with me for a couple of days.'

'But for what, Charlie?' asked Nora with real interest.

'For what?' repeated Charlie in surprise. Charlie was under the illusion most common among his countrymen that his meaning was always crystal-clear. 'Nora,' he went on with a touch of pathos, 'I'll be frank with you. You're the only one I can be frank with. You're the only friend I have in the world. My position is hopeless. Hopeless! Father Ring said it himself. "Marrying a girl with doubts like that, what can you expect,

Charlie?" There's only one thing that would break the spell – have the honeymoon first and the marriage after.'

It was dark, but he watched her closely from under the peak of his cap and saw that he had knocked her flat. No one had ever discussed such a subject with Nora before.

'But wouldn't it be a terrible sin, Charlie?' she asked with a quaver in her voice.

'Not if 'twas done with a good object,' Charlie said firmly, answering her out of her own mouth.

'I'm sure she'd do it even without that, Charlie,' Nora said with sudden bitterness.

'If she loved me she would,' said Charlie hopefully.

'Love?' cried Nora scornfully, springing from her chair, all her maiden airs dropping from her and leaving her a mature, raging, jealous woman. 'Don't be deceiving yourself like that, my dear man. That one doesn't love you.'

'What? Who? Who doesn't love me?' asked Charlie in stupefaction.

It was her turn then.

'Weren't you talking about Molly O'Regan?' she asked in alarm.

'Molly O'Regan?' Charlie cried, raising his face to the ceiling like a dog about to bay. 'What the hell put Molly O'Regan into your head, woman? Sure, I could have Molly O'Regan in the morning and the child along with her. Isn't that what I was saying to you?'

'Oh,' said Nora, drawing back from him with a look of horror, 'don't say any more!'

'But my God, girl,' moaned Charlie, thinking of his beauti-ful scene absolutely wasted and impossible to begin on again, 'sure you must know I don't give a snap of my fingers for Molly O'Regan! You were the first woman I ever gave a damn about, only you wouldn't have me. I only married Polly because she was your shadow. Even Father Ring knew that.'

'Oh,' she cried as if she were just ready to go into hysterics, 'I couldn't do it! I couldn't!'

'No, no, no, no,' said Charlie in alarm as though such an idea

had never crossed his mind. 'You're taking me up wrong.
Whisht, now, whisht, or you'll be heard!'

'You must never, never say such a thing to me again,' she
said, looking at him as though he were a devil in human shape.

'But my God, woman,' he cried indignantly, 'I didn't.
You're missing the whole point. I never asked you. I said if you
were a different sort of woman I might ask you. I was only
putting the case the way I put it to Father Ring. Surely you
can understand that?'

It seemed she couldn't, not altogether anyhow, and Charlie
strode to the door, his hands clasped behind his back and a
gloomy look on his face.

'I'm sorry if I upset you,' he snapped over his shoulder. ' 'Tis
your own fault didn't marry me first. You're the only woman
I ever cared about and I wanted to explain.'

She was staring at him incredulously, brushing back the
loose black hair from her forehead with an uncertain hand. She
looked childish and beautiful. If Charlie had only known, she
was thinking what a very queer way the Holy Ghost had
answered her prayer. As Polly had once said the Lord's ways
were very peculiar. Charlie waited for some sign of relenting in
her but saw none and, heaving a deep sigh, he left. Crossing
the bridge when the abbey tower was all black and spiky against
the sky and the lights in the back of the little shops were re-
flected in the river, he was like a man demented. He had done
it again! This time he'd done it for good. It would soon be in
everyone's mouth that he had tried to seduce a second girl. He
knew how it would be interpreted. He saw it already like head-
lines in a newspaper: WELL-KNOWN SHOPKEEPER'S SHOCKING
PROPOSAL OUTRAGED FATHER'S INDIGNATION. The girl who
had stood by him when no one else would do it – this was her
thanks! And it all came of Romeo and Juliet, the Captain's
Daughter and the rest of the nonsense. There was a curse on
him. Nora would tell her father and Father Ring; between
them they would raise up a host of new enemies against him;
no one would do business with him – a foolish, idle, dreamy,
impractical man!

11

He let a week go by before he did anything. In that time he realized the full horror of the scrape he had got himself into, and avoided every contact with people he knew. He spent most of his time in the sitting-room, and only went down to the shop when the girl came up for him and he knew that the visitor was a genuine customer and not an angel of vengeance. Finally, he asked Jim O'Regan in for a drink.

Jim was an ex-soldier, small, gaunt, and asthmatic, dressed in a blue serge suit that was no bluer than his face and with a muffler high about his throat. Johnny Desmond gave them a queer look as they entered, but Charlie, seemingly in the highest spirits, rattled away about everything till it dawned on them both that he had opened negotiations for Molly and the child. Charlie could have gone further but once glance at Jim's mean poker face and he remembered the scene outside the graveyard, and then it was as if Holy Ireland, Romeo and Juliet, and all the romantic dreams of his youth started with a cry from their slumber. It was terrible, but he couldn't help it; he was an unfortunate dreamy man.

Later that morning he had to go to the bank. The whole week he had been putting it off, but he could put it off no longer. He gave a quick glance up the street to see that the coast was clear and then strode briskly out. He hadn't gone a hundred yards when he saw Jerry Lawlor coming down the same pavement. Charlie looked round frantically for some lane or shop he could take refuge in but there was none. 'Brass, boys, brass!' he groaned. But to his great surprise Jerry showed no signs of anger, only a slight surprise at Charlie's slinking air.

'Good morrow, Charlie,' he said, sticking his thumbs in the armholes of his vest, 'as you won't say it yourself,' he added jovially.

'Oh, good morrow, good morrow, Jerry,' cried Charlie with false heartiness, trying to read the signs on Jerry's battered countenance. 'Up to the bank I'm rushing,' he said confidentially.

'The bank?' Jerry said slyly. 'Not the presbytery?'

'What the hell would I be doing at the presbytery?' Charlie exclaimed with a watchful smile.

'Oh, headquarters, headquarters,' replied Jerry. 'Who was it was telling me you were thinking of taking the field again? I believe your patrols were out.'

'Patrols, Jerry?' Charlie echoed in surprise. 'Ah, I'm too old for soldiering.'

'I hope not, Charlie,' said Jerry. 'Begor,' he added, squaring his shoulders, 'I don't know that I'd mind shouldering the old shotgun again in a good cause. Well, be good!' he ended with a wink and a nod.

He left Charlie open-mouthed on the pavement, looking after him. What the blazes did Jerry Lawlor mean? he wondered, scratching his poll. 'Be good' – was that the sort of advice you'd expect from a man whose daughter you had just been trying to seduce? 'Be good' – was the man mad or something? He couldn't understand why Jerry, who had the devil's own temper, took his advances to Nora in that spirit. Was it possible that Nora had censored them so much that he hadn't understood? Was it – a wild hope – that she hadn't told him at all? His face fell again. No woman could keep a thing like that to herself. If she hadn't told her father, she'd told someone else, and sooner or later it would get back to him. He heaved a bitter sigh. The sooner he could fix up things with the O'Regans the sooner he would be armed to face the attack.

He went on, but his luck seemed to be dead out that morning. As he went in the door Father Ring came out. Charlie gave him a terrified look, but before he could even think of escape, Father Ring was shaking his hand.

'You're looking well, Charlie.'

'I'm not feeling too good, Father,' said Charlie, thinking how far from the truth it was.

'Tell me,' said Father Ring confidentially, 'you didn't do any more about that little matter we were discussing?'

'To tell you the truth, Father,' Charlie said with apparent candour, 'I didn't.'

'Take your time,' Father Ring said with a knowing look. 'There's no hurry. I wouldn't be surprised if something could be done about that kid of yours. Mind! I'm not making any promises, but there's a soft corner there for you all right, and the father wouldn't let her go empty-handed. You know what I mean?'

'I do, Father,' groaned Charlie, meaning that he hadn't a notion, and as Father Ring went round the corner towards the church he stood on the bank steps with his head in a whirl. It was a spring day, a sunshiny day which made even the Main Street look cheerful, but Charlie was too confused for external impressions. For a week he had skulked like an assassin from Jerry Lawlor and Father Ring, yet here they treated him like lovers. And Nora went to confession to Father Ring! Admitting that he wouldn't let on what she did tell him, he couldn't conceal what she didn't, and it was quite plain that she hadn't told either of them about Charlie. Now what purpose would a girl have in concealing a thing like that? Modesty? But modesty in Charlie's mind was associated with nothing but hullabaloo. There was another flash of hope like a firework in his head, and then again darkness. 'Christ!' he thought despairingly. 'I'm going dotty! 'Tis giving up the drink in such a hurry.'

'Morra, Charlie,' said a farmer going in, but Charlie didn't even acknowledge the salute. His face was screwed up like that of a man who has forgotten what he came for. Then he drew a deep breath, pulled himself erect, and set off at a brisk pace for the Lawlors'.

Nora came out when she heard him banging on the door and gaped at him with horror-stricken eyes. He pushed her rudely back into the kitchen before him.

'Sit down, sit down!' he said shortly.

'What would I sit down for?' she asked in a low voice, and then her knees seemed to give way and she flopped.

'When can you marry me?' asked Charlie, standing over her like a boxer, ready to knock her flat if she rose again.

'Why?' she asked in a dead voice. 'Wouldn't Molly O'Regan have you?'

'Ha, ha,' laughed Charlie bitterly. 'I see the tomtoms were working this morning.'

'I suppose you think we don't know that 'tis all arranged?' she asked, throwing back her head to toss aside the stray curl that fell across her face.

'The trouble with you,' Charlie said vindictively, 'is that you always know other people's business and never know your own. When you met the one man that cared for you you let him slip. That's how much you knew. You're trying to do the same thing now.'

'If you cared for me you wouldn't ask me to disrespect myself,' she said with mournful accusation.

'If I didn't, I wouldn't ask you at all,' snapped Charlie. 'Now, I'm asking you properly. Once and for all, will you marry me?'

'But why should you?' she asked in a vague hysterical tone, rising with her hands thrown out and her head well back. 'You know now the sort of woman I am. You need never respect me any more.'

'What the hell is up with you?' shouted Charlie, almost dancing with fury. Whatever he said to this girl seemed to be wrong.

'There's nothing up with me,' she answered in a reasonable tone which was as close to lunacy as anything Charlie had ever heard. 'I know what I am now – that's all.'

'And what are you?' asked Charlie in alarm.

'You ought to know,' she said triumphantly. 'I didn't slap your face, did I?'

'You didn't what?' cried Charlie with an agonized look.

'Oh,' she cried in a rapture of self-abasement, 'I deceived myself nicely all the years. I thought I was a good-living woman but you knew better. You knew what I was; a cheap, vulgar, sensual woman that you could say what you liked to. Or do what you liked to. I suppose it's the just punishment for my pride. Why would you marry me when you can get me for nothing?'

Charlie had another flash of inspiration, this time inspiration mixed with pity and shame. He suddenly saw the girl was fond of him and would do anything for him. Jessica, Juliet, the Captain's Daughter, the whole blooming issue. This was the real thing, the thing he had always been looking for and never found. He nearly swept her off her feet as he grabbed her.

'God forgive me!' he said thickly. 'The finest woman in Ireland and I tormenting you like that! Your father and the priest have more sense than me. Put on your things and we'll go down and see them.'

'No, no, no,' she cried hysterically like a Christian martyr offering herself to the lions. 'Your mother said I'd never rock a cradle for you.'

'My mother, my mother – she has me as bad as herself. Never mind what she says.'

'But what'll you do if she puts spells on me?' she asked in a dazed tone, putting her hand to her forehead.

'Roast her over a slow fire,' snapped Charlie. He was himself again, aged seventeen, a roaring revolutionary and rationalist, ready to take on the British Empire, the Catholic Church, and the Wise Woman all together. 'Now listen to me, girl,' he said, taking her hands. 'No one is going to put spells on you. And no one is going to haunt you, either. That's only all old women's talk and we had enough of it to last us our lives. We're a match for anyone and anything. Now, what are you doing?'

'Making the dinner,' said Nora, blinking and smiling at anything so prosaic.

'We'll have dinner in town, the four of us,' said Charlie. 'Now come on!'

He stood behind her grinning as she put on her hat. She put it on crooked and her face was blotched beyond anything a powder-puff could repair, but Charlie didn't mind. He felt grand. At last he had got what he had always wanted, and he knew the rest would come. (It did too, and all Mrs Cashman's spells didn't delay it an hour.) As for Nora, she had no notion what she had got, but she had an alarming suspicion that it was the very opposite of what she had always desired.

(Which, for a woman, is usually more or less the same thing.)

A Bachelor's Story

Every old bachelor has a love story in him if only you can get at it. This is usually not very easy because a bachelor is a man who does not lightly trust his neighbour, and by the time you can identify him as what he is, the cause of it all has been elevated into a morality, almost a divinity, something the old bachelor himself is almost afraid to look at for fear it might turn out to be stuffed. And woe betide you if he does confide in you, and you by word or look suggest that you do think it is stuffed, for that is how my own friendship with Archie Boland ended.

Archie was a senior civil servant, a big man with a broad red face and hot blue eyes and a crust of worldliness and bad temper overlaying a nature that had a lot of sweetness and fun in it. He was a man who affected to believe the worst of everyone, but he saw that I appreciated his true character, and suppressed his bad temper most of the time except when I trespassed on his taboos, religious and political. For years the two of us walked home together. We both loved walking, and we both liked to drop in at a certain pub by the canal bridge where they kept good draught stout. Whenever we encountered some woman we knew Archie was very polite and even effusive in an old-fashioned way, raising his hat with a great sweeping gesture and bowing low over the hand he held as if he were about to kiss it, which I swear he would have done on the least encouragement. But afterwards he would look at me under his eyebrows with a knowing smile and tell me things about their home life which the ladies would have been very distressed to hear, and this in turn would give place to a sly look that implied that I was drawing my own conclusions from what he said, which I wasn't, not usually.

'I know what you think, Delaney,' he said one evening, carefully putting down the two pints and lowering himself heavily into his seat. 'You think I'm a bad case of sour grapes.'

'I wasn't thinking anything at all,' I said.

'Well, maybe you mightn't be too far wrong at that,' he conceded, more to his own view of me than to anything else. 'But it's not only that, Delaney. There are other things involved. You see, when I was your age I had an experience that upset me a lot. It upset me so much that I felt I could never go through the same sort of thing again. Maybe I was too idealistic.'

I never heard a bachelor yet who didn't take a modest pride in his own idealism. And there in the far corner of that pub by the canal bank on a rainy autumn evening, Archie took the plunge and told me the story of the experience that had turned him against women, and I put my foot in it and turned him against me as well. Ah, well, I was younger then!

You see, in his earlier days Archie had been a great cyclist. Twice he had cycled round Ireland and had made any amount of long trips to see various historic spots, battlefields, castles and cathedrals. He was no scholar, but he liked to know what he was talking about and had no objection to showing other people that they didn't. 'I suppose you know that place you were talking about, James?' he would purr when someone in the office stuck his neck out. 'Because if you don't, I do.' No wonder he wasn't too popular with the staff.

One evening Archie arrived in a remote Connemara village where four women teachers were staying, studying Irish, and after supper he got to chatting with them and they all went for a walk along the strand. One was a young woman called Madge Hale, a slight girl with blue-grey eyes, a long clear-skinned face and a rather breathless manner, and Archie did not take long to see that she was altogether more intelligent than the others, and that whenever he said something interesting her whole face lit up like a child's.

The teachers were going on a trip to the Aran Islands next day, and Archie offered to join them. They visited the tiny oratories, and as none of the teachers knew anything about these, Archie in his well-informed way described the origin of the island monasteries and the life of the hermit monks in the early medieval period. Madge was fascinated and kept asking questions about what the churches had looked like, and Archie, flattered into doing the dog, suggested that she should accompany him on a bicycle trip the following day, and see some of the later monasteries. She agreed at once enthusiastically. The other women laughed, and Madge laughed too, though it was clear that she didn't really know what they were laughing about.

Now this was one sure way to Archie's heart. He disliked women because they were always going to parties or the pictures, painting their faces and taking aspirin in cartloads. There was altogether too much nonsense about them for a man of his grave taste, but at last he had met a girl who seemed absolutely devoid of nonsense and was serious through and through.

Their trip next day was a great success and he was able to point out to her the development of the monastery church through the medieval abbey to the preaching church. That evening when they returned, he suggested, half in jest, that she should borrow the bicycle and come back to Dublin with him. This time she hesitated, but it was only for a few moments as she considered the practical end of it, and then her face lit up in the same eager way and she said in her piping voice: 'If you think I won't be in your way, Archie.'

Now she was in Archie's way, and very much in his way, for he was a man of old-fashioned ideas who had never in his life allowed a woman he was accompanying to pay for as much as a cup of tea for herself, felt that to have to excuse himself on the road was little short of obscene, and endured the agonies of the damned when he had to go to a country hotel with a pretty girl at the end of the day. When he went to the reception desk he felt sure that everyone believed unmentionable things about him and had an overwhelming compulsion to lecture them on the subject of their evil imaginations. But for this too he admired her. By this time any other girl would have been wondering what her parents and friends would say if they knew she was spending the night in a country hotel with a man, but the very idea of scandal never seemed to enter Madge's head. And it was not, as he shrewdly divined, that she was either fast or flighty. It was merely that it had never occurred to her that anything she and Archie might do involved any culpability.

That settled Archie's business. He knew she was the only woman in the world for him, though to tell her this when she was more or less at the mercy of his solicitations was something that did not even cross his mind. He had a sort of old-fashioned chivalry that set him above the commoner temptations. They cycled south through Clare to Limerick, and stood on the cliffs overlooking the Atlantic; the weather held fine, and they drifted up through the flat apple country to Cashel and drank beer and lemonade in country pubs, and finally pushed over the hills to Kilkenny, where they spent their last evening wandering in the dusk under the ruins of medieval abbeys and inns, studying effigies and blazons; and never once did Archie as much as hold her hand or speak to her of love. He scowled as he told me this, as though I might mock him from the depths of my own small experience, but I had no inclination to do so, for I knew that enchantment of the senses that people of chaste and lonely character feel in one another's company and which haunts the memory more than all the passionate embraces of lovers.

When they separated outside Madge's lodgings in Rathmines late one summer evening. Archie felt that he was at last free to speak. He held her hand as he said goodbye.

'I think we had quite good fun, don't you?' he asked.

'Oh, yes, Archie,' she cried, laughing in her delight. 'It was wonderful. It was the happiest holiday I ever spent.'

He was so encouraged by this that he deliberately retained hold of her hand.

'That's the way I feel,' he said, beginning to blush. 'I didn't like to say it before because I thought you might not like it. I never met a woman like you before, and if you ever felt you wanted to marry me I'd be honoured.'

For a moment, as her face suddenly darkened as though all the delight had drained from it, he thought that he had embarrassed her even now.

'Are you sure, Archie?' she asked nervously. 'Because you

don't know me very long, remember. A few days like that is not enough to know a person.'

'That's a thing that soon rights itself,' Archie said oracularly.

'And besides, we'd have to wait a long while,' she added. 'My people aren't very well off; I have two brothers younger than me and I have to help them.'

'And I have a long way to go before I get anywhere in the Civil Service,' he replied good-humouredly, 'so it may be quite a while before I can do what I like as well. But those are things that also right themselves, and they right themselves all the sooner if you do them with an object in mind. I know my own character pretty well,' he added thoughtfully, 'and I know it would be a help to me. And I'm not a man to change his mind.'

She still seemed to hesitate; for a second or two he had a strong impression that she was about to refuse him, but then she thought better of it. Her face cleared in the old way, and she gave her nervous laugh.

'Very well, Archie,' she said. 'If you really want me, you'll find me willing.'

'I want you, Madge,' he replied gravely, and then he raised his hat and pushed his bicycle away while she stood outside her gate in the shadow of the trees and waved. I admired that gesture even as he described it. It was so like Archie, and I could see that such a plighting of his word would haunt him as no passionate lovemaking would ever do. It was magnificent, but it was not love. People should be jolted out of themselves at times like those, and when they are not so jolted it frequently means, as it did with Archie, that the experience is only deferred till a less propitious time.

However, he was too innocent to know anything of that. To him the whole fantastic business of walking out with a girl was miracle enough in itself, like being dumped down in the middle of some ancient complex civilization whose language and customs he was unfamiliar with. He might have introduced her to history, but she introduced him to operas and concerts, and in no time he was developing prejudices about music as though it was something that had fired him from boyhood, for Archie was by nature a Gospel-maker. Even when I knew him he shook his head over my weakness for Wagner. Bach was the man, and somehow Bach at once ceased to be a pleasure and became a responsibility. It was part of the process of what he called 'knowing his own mind'.

On fine Sundays in autumn they took their lunch and walked over the mountains to Enniskerry or cycled down the Boyne Valley to Drogheda. Madge was a girl of very sweet disposition so that they rarely had a falling-out, and even at the best of times this must have been an event in Archie's life, for he had an irascible, quarrelsome, Gospel-making streak. It was true that there were certain evenings and weekends that she kept to herself to visit her old friends and an ailing aunt in Miltown, but these did not worry Archie, who believed that this was how a conscientious girl should be. As a man who knew his own mind he liked to feel that the girl he was going to marry was the same.

Oh, of course it was too perfect! Of course, an older hand would have waited to see what price he was expected to pay for all those perfections, but Archie was an idealist, which meant that he thought Nature was in the job solely for his benefit. Then one day Nature gave him a rap on the knuckles just to show him that the boot was on the other foot.

In town he happened to run into one of the group of teachers he had met in Connemara during the holidays and invited her politely to join him in a cup of tea. Archie favoured one of those long mahogany tea-houses in Grafton Street where daylight never enters; but he was a creature of habit, and this was where he had eaten his first lunch in Dublin, and there he would continue to go till some minor cataclysm like marriage changed the current of his life.

'I hear you're seeing a lot of Madge,' said the teacher gaily, as if this were a guilty secret between herself and Archie.

'Oh, yes,' said Archie as if it weren't. 'And with God's help I expect to be doing the same for the rest of my life.'

'So I heard,' she said joyously. 'I'm delighted for Madge, of course. But I wonder whatever happened to that other fellow she was engaged to?'

'Why?' asked Archie, who knew well that she was only

pecking at him and refused to let her see how sick he felt. 'Was she engaged to another fellow?'

'Ah, surely she must have told you that!' the teacher cried with mock consternation. 'I hope I'm not saying anything wrong,' she added piously. 'Maybe she wasn't engaged to him after all. He was a teacher too, I believe – somewhere on the south side. What was his name?'

'I'll ask her and let you know,' replied Archie blandly. He was giving nothing away till he had more time to think of it.

All the same he was in a very ugly temper. Archie was one of those people who believe in being candid with everybody, even at the risk of unpleasantness, which might be another reason that he had so few friends when I knew him. He might, for instance, hear from somebody called Mahony that another man called Devins had said he was inclined to be offensive in argument, which was a reasonable enough point of view, but Archie would feel it his duty to go straight to Devins and ask him to repeat the remark, which, of course, would leave Devins wondering who it was that had been trying to make mischief for him, so he would ask a third man whether Mahony was the tell-tale, and a fourth would repeat the question to Mahony, till eventually, I declare to God, Archie's inquisition would have the whole office by the ears.

Archie, of course, had felt compelled to confess to Madge every sin of his past life, which from the point of view of this narrative, was quite without importance, and he naturally assumed when Madge did not do the same thing that it could only be because she had nothing to confess. He realized now that this was a grave mistake since everyone has something to confess, particularly women.

He could have done with her what he would have done with someone in the office and asked her what she meant, but this did not seem sufficient punishment to him. Though he didn't recognize it, Archie's pride was deeply hurt. He regarded Madge's silence as equivalent to an insult, and in the matter of insults he felt it was his duty to give as good as he got. So, instead of having it out with her as another man might have done, he proceeded to make her life a misery. He continued to walk out with her as though nothing had happened and then brought the conversation round gently to various domestic disasters which had or had not occurred in his own experience and all of which had been caused solely by someone's deceit. This was intended to scare the wits out of Madge, as no doubt it did. Then he called up a friend of his in the Department of Education and asked him out for a drink.

'The Hale girl?' his friend said thoughtfully. 'Isn't she engaged to that assistant in St Joseph's? Wheeler, a chap with a lame leg? I think I heard that. Why? You're not keen on her yourself by any chance?'

'Ah, you know me,' Archie replied with a fat smile.

'Why then indeed, I do not,' said his friend. 'But if you mean business you'd want to hurry up. Now you mention it, they were only supposed to be waiting till he got a headship somewhere. He's a nice fellow, I believe.'

'So I'm told,' said Archie, and went away with a smile on his lips and murder in his heart. Those forthright men of the world are the very devil once they get a bee in their bonnets. Othello had nothing on a civil servant of twelve years' standing and a blameless reputation. So he still continued to see Madge, though now his method of tormenting her was to press her about those odd evenings she was supposed to spend with her aunt or those old friends she spoke of. He realized that some of those evenings were probably spent as innocently as she described spending them, since she showed neither embarrassment nor distress at his probing and gibing. It was the others that caused her to wince, and those were the ones he concentrated on.

'I could meet you when you came out, you know,' he said in a benign tone that almost glowed.

'But I don't know when I'll be out, Archie,' she replied, blushing and stammering.

'Ah, well, even if you didn't get out until half past ten – and that would be late for a lady her age – it would still give us time for a little walk. That's if the night was fine, of course. It's all very well doing your duty by old friends, but you don't want to deny yourself every little pleasure.'

'I couldn't promise anything, Archie, really I couldn't,' she said, almost angrily, and Archie smiled to himself, the smug smile of the old inquisitor whose helpless victim has begun to give himself away.

The road where Madge lived was one of those broad Victorian roads you find scattered all over the hills at the south side of Dublin, with trees along the pavement and deep gardens leading to pairs of semi-detached solidly built merchants' houses with tall basements and high flights of steps. Next night Archie was waiting at the corner of a side street in the shadow, feeling like a detective as he watched her house. He had been there only about ten minutes when she came out and tripped down the steps. When she emerged from the garden she turned right up the hill, and Archie followed, guided more by the distinctive clack of her heels than by the glimpses he caught of her passing swiftly under a street lamp.

She reached the bus stop at the top of the road and a man came up and spoke to her. He was a youngish man in a bright tweed coat, hatless and thin, dragging a lame leg. He took her arm and they went off together in the direction of the Dodder bank. As they did, Archie heard her happy, eager, foolish laugh, and it sounded exactly as though she were laughing at the thought of him.

He was beside himself with misery. He had got what he had been seeking, which was full confirmation of the woman's guilt, and now he had no idea what to do with it. To follow them and have it out on the riverbank in the darkness was one possibility, but he realized that Wheeler – if this was Wheeler – probably knew as little of him as he had known of Wheeler, and that it would result only in general confusion. No, it was that abominable woman he would have to have it out with. He returned slowly to his post, turned into a public-house just round the corner and sat swallowing whiskey in silence until another customer unwitting touched on one of his pet political taboos. Then he sprang to his feet, and though no one had invited his opinion, he thundered for several minutes against people with slave minds and stalked out with a virtuous feeling that his wrath had been entirely disinterested.

This time he had to wait for over half an hour in the damp and cold, and this did not improve his temper. Then he heard her footsteps and guessed that the young man had left her at the same spot where they had met. It could, of course, have been the most innocent thing in the world, intended merely to deceive some inquisitive people in her lodging-house, but to Archie it seemed all guile and treachery. He crossed the road and stood under a tree beside the gate, so well concealed that she failed altogether to see him till he stepped out to meet her. Then she started back.

'Who's that?' she asked in a startled whisper, and then, after a look, added with what sounded like joy and was probably merely relief: 'Oh, Archie, it's you!' Then, as he stood there glowering at her, her tone changed again and he could detect the consternation as she asked:

'What are you doing here, Archie?'

'Waiting,' Archie replied in a voice as hollow as his heart felt.

'Waiting? But for what, Archie?'

'An explanation.'

'Oh, Archie!' she exclaimed with childish petulance. 'Don't talk to me that way!'

'And what way would you like me to talk to you?' he retorted, letting fly with his anger. 'I suppose you're going to tell me now you were at your aunt's?'

'No, Archie,' she replied meekly. 'I wasn't. I was out with a friend.'

'A friend?' repeated Archie.

'Not a friend exactly either, Archie,' she added in distress.

'Not exactly,' Archie repeated with grim satisfaction. 'With your fiancé, in fact?'

'That's true, Archie,' she admitted. 'I don't deny that. You must let me explain.'

'The time for explanations is past,' Archie thundered magnificently, though the moment before he had been demanding one. 'The time for explanations was three months ago. For three months and more your whole life has been a living lie.'

This was a phrase Archie had thought up, entirely without assistance, drinking whiskey in the pub. He may have failed to notice that it was not entirely original. It was intended to draw blood and it did.

'I wish you wouldn't say things like that, Archie,' Madge said in an unsteady voice. 'I know I didn't tell you the whole truth, but I wasn't trying to deceive you.'

'No, of course you weren't trying,' said Archie. 'You don't need to try. What you ought to try some time is to tell the truth.'

'But I am telling the truth,' she said indignantly. 'I'm not a liar, Archie, and I won't have you saying it. I couldn't help getting engaged to Pat. He asked me and I couldn't refuse him.'

'You couldn't refuse him?'

'No. I told you you should let me explain. It happened before and I won't have it happen again.'

'What happened?'

'Oh, it's a long story, Archie. I once refused a boy at home in our own place and – he died.'

'He died?' Archie said incredulously.

'Well, he committed suicide. It was an awful thing to happen, but it wasn't my fault. I was young and silly, and I didn't know how dangerous it was. I thought it was just all a game, and I led him on and made fun of him. How could I know the way a boy would feel about things like that?'

'Hah!' Archie grunted uncertainly, feeling that as usual she had thought too quickly for him, and that all his beautiful anger accumulated over weeks would be wasted on some pointless argument. 'And I suppose you felt you couldn't refuse me either?'

'Well, as a matter of fact, Archie,' she said apologetically, 'that was the way I felt.'

'Good God!' exploded Archie.

'It's true, Archie,' she said in a rush. 'It wasn't until weeks after that I got to like you really, the way I do now. I was hoping all that time we were together that you didn't like me that way at all, and it came as a terrible blow to me, Archie. Because, as you see, I was sort of engaged already, and it's not a situation you'd like to be in yourself, being engaged to two girls at the one time.'

'And I suppose you thought I'd commit suicide?' Archie asked incredulously.

'But I didn't know, Archie. It wasn't until afterwards that I really got to know you.'

'You didn't know!' he said, choking with anger at the suggestion that he was a man of such weak and commonplace stuff. 'You didn't *know*! Good God, the vanity and madness of it! And all this time you couldn't tell me about the fellow you say committed suicide on account of you.'

'But how could I, Archie?' she asked despairingly. 'It's not the sort of thing a girl likes to think of, much less to talk about.'

'No,' he said, breathing deeply, 'and so you'll go through life, tricking and deceiving every honourable man that comes your way — all out of pure kindness of heart. That be damned for a yarn!'

'It's not a yarn, Archie,' she cried hotly. 'It's true, and it never happened with anyone only Pat and you, and one young fellow at home, but the last I heard of him he was walking out with another girl, and I dare say he's over it by now. And Pat would have got over it the same if only you'd had patience.'

The picture of yet a third man engaged to his own fiancée was really too much for Archie, and he knew that he could never stand up to this little liar in argument.

'Madge,' he said broodingly, 'I do not like to insult any woman to her face, least of all a woman I once respected, but I do not believe you. I can't believe anything you say. You have behaved to me in a deceitful and dishonourable manner, and I can't trust you any longer.'

Then he turned on his heel and walked heavily away, remembering how on this very spot, a few months before, he had turned away with his heart full of hope, and he realized that everything people said about women was true down to the last bitter gibe, and that never again would he trust one of them.

'That was the end of my attempts at getting married,' he finished grimly. 'Of course, she wrote and gave me the names of two witnesses I could refer to if I didn't believe her, but I couldn't even be bothered replying.'

'Archie,' I asked in consternation, 'you don't mean that you really dropped her?'

'Dropped her?' he repeated, beginning to scowl. 'I never spoke to the woman again, only to raise my hat to her whenever I met her on the street. I don't even know what happened to her after, whether she married or not. I have some pride.'

'But, Archie,' I said despairingly, 'suppose she was simply telling the truth?'

'And suppose she was?' he asked in a murderous tone.

Then I began to laugh. I couldn't help it, though I saw it was making him mad. It was raining outside on the canal bank, and I wasn't laughing at Archie so much as at myself. Because for the first time I found myself falling in love with a woman from the mere description of her, as they do in the old romances, and it was an extraordinary feeling, as though there existed somewhere some pure essence of womanhood that one could savour outside the body.

'But damn it, Archie,' I cried, 'you said yourself she was a serious girl. All you're telling me now is that she was a sweet one as well. It must have been hell for her, being engaged to two men in the same town and trying to keep both of them happy till one got tired of her and left her free to marry you.'

'Or free for a third man to come along and put her in the same position again,' said Archie with a sneer.

I must say I had not expected that one, and for a moment it stopped me dead. But there is no stopping a man who is in love with a shadow as I was then, and I was determined on finding justification for myself.

'But after all, Archie,' I said, 'isn't that precisely why you marry a woman like that? Can you imagine marrying one of them if the danger wasn't there? Come, Archie, don't you see that the whole business of the suicide is irrelevant? Every nice girl behaves exactly as though she had a real suicide in her past. That's what makes her a nice girl. It's not easy to defend it rationally, but that's the way it is. Archie, I think you made a fool of yourself.'

'It's not possible to defend it rationally or any other way,' Archie said with finality. 'A woman like that is a woman without character. You might as well stick your head in a gas oven and be done with it as marry a girl like that.'

And from that evening on, Archie dropped me. He even told his friends that I had no moral sense, and would be bound to end up bad. Perhaps he was right; perhaps I shall end up as badly as he believed, but, on the other hand, perhaps I was only saying to him all the things he had been saying to himself for years in the bad hours coming on to morning, and he only wanted reassurance from me, not his own sentence on himself pronounced by another man's lips. But, as I say, I was very young and didn't understand. Nowadays I should sympathize and congratulate him on his narrow escape and leave it to him to proclaim what an imbecile he was.

The House that Johnny Built

Every morning about the same time Johnny Desmond came to the door of his shop for a good screw up and down the street. He was like an old cat stretching himself after a nap. He had his cap down over his left eye and his hands in his trouser pockets, and first he inspected the sky, then the Square end of Main Street, then the abbey end, and finally there were a lot of small personal stares at other shops and at people who passed. Johnny owned the best general store in town, a man who came in from the country without, as you might say, a boot to his foot. He had a red face, an apoplectic face which looked like a plum pudding you'd squeezed up and down till it bulged sideways, so that the features were all flattened and spread out and the two eyes narrowed into slits. As if that was not enough he looked at you from under the peak of his cap as though you were the headlights of a car, his right eye cocked, his left screwed up, till his whole face was as wrinkled as a roasted apple.

Now, one morning as Johnny looked down towards the abbey, what should he see but a handsome woman in a white coat coming up towards him with her head bowed and her hands in her coat pockets. She was a woman he had never before, to his knowledge, laid eyes on, and he stared at her and saluted, and then stood looking after her with his left eye closed as though he were still a bit blinded by her headlights.

'Tom!' he called without looking round.

'Yes, Mr D.?' said his assistant from behind the counter.

'Who's that, Tom?' asked Johnny, knowing he needn't specify.

'That's the new doctor,' said Tom.

'Doctor?' echoed Johnny, swinging his head right round.

'Doctor O'Brien in the dispensary.'

'Which O'Briens are they, Tom?' asked Johnny in a baffled tone.

'Micky the Miser,' said Tom.

'Micky of Asragh?' exclaimed Johnny, as if it were too much for human reason.

Every morning after that he waited for her, and even strode up the street alongside her, rolling along like a barrel on props and jingling the coin in his trouser pocket.

'Tom!' he called when he returned.

'Yes, Mr D.?'

'There's style for you!' grunted Johnny.

'She can damn well afford it,' grunted Tom.

'There's breeding for you!' said Johnny.

'She's a bitch for her beer,' said Tom.

But beer or no beer – and Johnny had a light hand on the liquor himself – he was impressed. He was more than impressed; he was inspired. He ordered a new brown suit and a new soft hat, put on a new gold watch-chain, and set off one night for the doctor's digs. They showed him into the parlour. Parlours always fascinated Johnny. Leave alone the furniture, which is a book in itself, a roomful of photos will set up a man of inquiring mind for life.

The doctor came in, a bit bosomy in a yellow blouse, and Johnny saw with interest and amusement that at the very first glance she took in the gold chain. She was a shy sort of girl, and the most you got from her as a rule was a hasty glance, but that same would blister you. He liked that in her. He liked a girl not to be a fool.

'I suppose you're surprised to see me?' said Johnny.

'I'm delighted, of course,' she said in a high singsong, the way they speak in Asragh. 'I hope there's nothing the matter?'

'Well, now,' said Johnny, who was by the way of being a bit of a joker, 'you put your finger on it. 'Tis the old heart.'

'Is it codding me you are?' she asked with a shocked look, her head bowed.

'Oh, the devil a cod,' said Johnny, delighted with his reception. 'I came to you because there's no one else I'd trust.'

"'Tis probably indigestion,' she said. 'Are you sleeping all right?'

'Poorly,' said Johnny.

'Is it palpitations?'

'Thumps,' said Johnny, indicating how his heart went pit-a-pat.

'Go to God!' she exclaimed, drawing down the blind a little and giving an inquisitive look down the street at the same time. 'Open that old shirt and give us a look at you.'

'I'd be too shy,' said Johnny drawing back in mock alarm.

'Shy, my nanny!' she exclaimed. 'What old nonsense you have! Will you open it before I drag it off you?'

'And besides,' Johnny said confidentially, 'what's wrong with my heart wouldn't show through the speaking-tube. Sit down there till I be talking to you.'

'Ah, botheration to you and your old jokes!' she cried in exasperation. 'Will you have a drop of whiskey? – though God knows you don't deserve it.'

'Whiskey?' chuckled Johnny, well pleased with the success of his act. 'What's that? Give us a drop till I try it?'

As she poured out the whiskey Johnny took out his cigarettes, and at once her eye was caught by the silver case – a girl in a thousand!

'That's a new cigarette-case you have,' she said. 'Is it silver?'

'' 'Tis,' said Johnny.

'Ah, God, Johnny,' she said, screwing up her eyes as she struck a light, 'you must be rolling in money.'

'I am,' said Johnny.

'Aren't you the selfish old devil wouldn't share it with some poor woman?'

'I'm coming to that,' said Johnny.

He took the tumbler from her, put one thumb in the arm-hole of his vest and waited till she sat down on the sofa, her goldy-brown hair coming loose and the finest pair of legs in the county tucked under her. Then he leaned back in his chair and gave his mouth a wiggle to limber it up.

'I'm fifty,' he said to the fire-screen. 'Fifty or near it,' he added to herself. 'I'm a well-to-do man. I never had a day's sickness, barring one rupture I got about twelve years ago. 'Twas the way I was lugging an old packing-case from the shop to the van.'

'Was it an operation you had?' she asked with professional curiosity.

' 'Twas.'

'Was it Caulfield did it?'

'That fellow!' Johnny said contemptuously. 'I wouldn't leave him sew on a button for me. I had Surgeon Hawthorne. Forty guineas he charged me.'

'Forty?' she exclaimed. 'He saw you coming.'

'And sixteen for the nursing home,' Johnny added bitterly. 'I wish I could make my money as easy. But anyway, between the jigs and the reels, I never thought much about marriage, and besides, the women in this town wouldn't suit me at all.' He let his chair fall back into position and leaned across the table towards her, his glass to one side, his pudgy hands clasped before him. 'The sort of man I am, I like a woman with a bit of style, and the women in this town that have style have no nature, and the ones that have nature have no style. I declare to my God,' he burst out indignantly, waving one hand in the air, 'whatever the hell they do to them in convent schools you couldn't get a laugh out of them. They're killed with grandeur. But you're different. You have the nature and you have the style.'

'Ah, hold on, Johnny!' cried the doctor in alarm. 'What ails you? 'Tisn't asking me to marry you you are?'

'If 'tisn't that same, 'tis no less,' said Johnny stoutly.

'Why then, I'll do nothing of the sort,' she retorted with the Asragh lilt in her voice like a dive-bomber swooping and soaring; as pretty a tune as ever you'd hear in the mouth of a good-looking girl unless she actually happened to be pitching you to blazes. 'Sure, God Almighty, Johnny, you're old enough to be my father.'

'If I'm older I'm steadier,' said Johnny, not liking the turn the conversation was taking.

'Like the Rock of Cashel,' she said cuttingly. 'But I never had much of a smack for history.'

'Now, what you ought to do,' said Johnny cunningly, 'is to talk to your father. See what advice will he give you. He's the smartest businessman in this part of the world, and the man that says it is no fool.'

'Ah, Johnny, will you have a bit of sense?' she begged. 'Sure, that sort of family haggling is over and done with these fifty years. You wouldn't get a girl in the whole county to let her father put a halter round her neck like that.'

'Are you sure now?' asked Johnny, feeling he might be just a little behind the times.

'Ah, of course I'm sure. God Almighty, Johnny,' she added, with the same dive-bomber swoop in her voice, 'isn't it the one little bit of pleasure we have?'

'I see, I see,' muttered Johnny, meaning that he didn't, and he stood up, dug his hands in his trouser pockets, and spun on one leg, studying the pattern in the carpet.

'Of course,' he went on in torment, 'you might be misled about what I'm worth. I'm worth a lot of money. Even your friend the bank manager doesn't know all I'm worth. No, nor half it.'

'Ah, Con Doody never even mentioned your name to me,' she said furiously, jumping up and giving him a glare. 'Sure, I wouldn't give a snap of my fingers for all your old money.'

'And you won't ask your father?'

'What a thing I'd do!'

'There's no harm done so,' Johnny said stiffly. 'You'll excuse my asking.'

And off he went in a huff. Next morning when she passed on her way to the dispensary, there was no sign of him. That vexed her, because she was just beginning to be sorry for not having taken him easier, and she worked herself up into such a temper that she told all about it at the bridge party that evening.

'And I declare to God,' she concluded innocently, 'he went out the door on me as if I was a bad neighbour that wouldn't give him the loan of my flatiron.'

2

But at the same time you couldn't help admiring Johnny's obstinacy. He was the sort who can do without something all the days of their lives, but from the moment the idea occurs to them, it gives them no peace. A month passed; two months passed; Johnny, everything awake in him, never stopped brooding and planning. And finally he went to John O'Connor, the County Council architect.

'Tell me,' he said, leaning his two arms on the table, his left eye screwed up and his lower lip thrust out, 'the couple of old houses I have there at the corner of the Skehenagh Road — what sort of place could you make of them?'

'Begor, I don't know, Johnny,' O'Connor said blandly, 'unless you were thinking of giving them to the National Museum.'

'I'm thinking of knocking them down,' said Johnny grimly.

'I see,' said O'Connor, sitting back and folding his hands. 'You could do a nice little job there all right if you had the tenants.'

'Never mind about the tenants,' said Johnny. 'What I'm thinking of is a shop.'

'What sort of shop?' O'Connor asked with new interest.

'That's for me to know and you to find out,' retorted Johnny with a chuckle. 'I want a new shop and a new house.'

'And I suppose I have to find out what sort of house you want as well?' O'Connor asked innocently.

'How many rooms would there be in that house of the bank manager's?' asked Johnny.

'Doody's!' O'Connor exclaimed. 'But that's a big place, man.'

'You couldn't swing a cat in that old place I have now,' said Johnny.

'I see,' said O'Connor dryly. ' 'Tis cats you're going in for.'

But it wasn't cats Johnny was going in for at all, but chemistry. A chemist's shop, if you please! And Johnny a man that never in his life sold more in that line than a cake of soap or a bottle of castor oil. The funny thing was that no one seemed to see that it might have anything to do with the doctor. The true grandeur of Johnny's fantasy was something beyond the conception of the town.

The house was a handsome affair. O'Connor got a free hand with everything, furniture and all, and he might have chosen the pictures as well, only that by way of a joke he suggested a lot of Old Masters as being suitable for an old bachelor. That settled it. Johnny didn't like being reminded of his failure with the doctor, so he said explosively that he was in no hurry; the pictures could wait.

He had the car to the station the night the new chemist arrived. She was a very pretty girl, just out of training, and with a nice, pleasing, unaffected air. Johnny had selected her himself from among a half-dozen candidates, principally for her manners, and he was glad to see that he had been right about these. Affectation in girls was the one thing Johnny couldn't stand; he said it frightened customers away.

All that day he had been driving himself and the maid crazy seeing that everything in the house was right for the new chemist; flowers on her dressing-table, the towels fresh, the water boiling. When Johnny was that way he was like a hen with an egg, poking round the kitchen and picking things up to ask what they were for. While the girl was upstairs he walked from one room to another and stopped in the hall with his head cocked to hear what she was up to now. He was waiting for her in the hall when she came down. She was looking grand. No wonder she would, after all the stories she had heard of the awful lives of chemists in Irish small towns.

'Was everything all right?' growled Johnny.

'Oh, grand, Mr Desmond, thanks,' she said cheerfully.

'Be sure and ask if there's anything you want,' he added. 'The girl is new. She might forget. You'll have a drop of sherry?'

'I'd love it,' she said and went into the sitting-room with him. O'Connor had furnished it beautifully. She warmed her hands while Johnny filled out the drinks.

'Here's health!' he said.

'Good health!' she replied and chuckled. 'A good job Daddy can't see me now.'

'Why's that?' asked Johnny.

'The poor man has no notion that I ever take a drink,' she said. 'If he had his way, we'd never be let do anything. He won't even have a book in the house unless 'tis by a priest, and he makes us be in every night by ten. He's in for a surprise one of these days.'

'I see I'll have to keep you in order,' said Johnny, but he didn't really hear more than half she was saying. He was thinking too much about the supper. At table he gave her more wine, red wine this time, and the result was that she continued to improve. The more she drank the more ladylike she became.

'Isn't Mrs Desmond well?' she asked at last in a confidential tone and with great concern.

'Mrs Desmond?' chuckled Johnny. 'Who's that?' He was beginning to feel easier, and thanked God sincerely that the meat part of it was over — a mistake wouldn't matter so much with the sweet.

'Your wife, I mean,' said the chemist.

'Ah, 'tis only the job in the shop that's filled,' laughed Johnny, feeling the wine warm him up. 'The other one is still vacant.'

'You mean you're not married?' asked the chemist.

'Aren't I great?' said Johnny.

'You're wonderful,' said the chemist, but a less enthusiastic man would have noticed there was something wrong in her tone. Johnny didn't even notice how her chatter dried up. He was talking too much himself. Supper had gone off splendidly, and when they went to the sitting-room for coffee he was beginning to get into his stride. Johnny's knowledge was personal and peculiar, when he chose to share it, which wasn't often, and a student of the social sciences would have got rare value out of his talk. Holding a cigarette in the hollow of his hand like a candle in a turnip, he strode up and down the room, holding forth about the shop he had made his money in and how he'd done it, and about the rival chemist's shop, which would prove no rival at all, for it was run by a poor benighted banshee of a man with no business sense. Johnny had it all taped. He told her about the doctors in the town. 'Woolley and Hyde and a woman doctor called O'Brien. Her father is a rich man. I dare say 'twas he got it for her.'

It gave him a certain satisfaction to get his own back like this on Doctor O'Brien, but the chemist didn't seem to be listening as carefully as you'd expect.

'You wouldn't mind if I run down to the chapel to say a little prayer, Mr Desmond?' she asked suddenly.

'The chapel?' Johnny echoed in astonishment, for his brain didn't adjust itself too rapidly and it was now going full speed ahead in another direction.

'I won't be a minute.'

' 'Tis raining cats and dogs, girl,' he said crossly. 'You'd be drenched. Wait a minute and I'll run you down in the car.'

'Oh, no, no, you mustn't do that,' she said hastily, clasping her hands. 'It's the air I wants as much as anything else. Really, I won't be a minute.'

'Oh, just as you like,' growled Johnny, flustered and hot and upset. He could have sworn that there was nothing in the world wrong with that supper. He stood in the hall as she went out in the rain, peered after her down the street and shouted: 'Don't be long!' His plum-pudding face was screwed up in mystification. Nine o'clock! What sense was there in that? He took up a paper and laid it down every time he heard a woman's step. The chapel was only a couple of hundred yards away. At ten he got up and began to prowl about the room with his hands in his pockets. The devil was in it if she didn't come home now, for the chapel shut at ten. The sweat broke out on him and he cursed himself and cursed his luck. The Town Hall clock struck eleven; he heard the maid go up to bed and surrendered himself to despair. Man or no man, eleven meant scandal. Nothing but misfortune ever came of women. What bad luck was on him the first day he saw a strange one in town? It was the doctor who was behind all his misfortunes.

Then he heard the sound of a car and his heart gave a jump. All the bad language he had been saving up for hours rose in him and, after one savage glance at the clock, he ran to the front door determined to give her a good lick of his tongue. The car was drawn up at the kerb, the engine stopped and the side-lights on. More blackguarding!

'Is that you?' he snarled, leaning out into the spitting rain.

'Why?' asked a familiar woman's voice. 'Were you waiting up for me?'

The door of the car opened and the doctor scuttled for shelter.

'Is there something up with the chemist?' he asked in holy terror, backing in before her.

'With who?' asked the doctor, screwing up her face in the bright light and pulling off her motoring gloves. 'I don't know what you're talking about. Aren't you going to ask whether we have a mouth on us?'

'There's whiskey on the sideboard,' snapped Johnny distractedly. 'Take it and leave me alone! I'm demented with the whole damn lot of ye. I thought you were the new chemist.'

'Wisha, Johnny,' asked the doctor in great concern as she filled her glass, 'is this the sort of hours she's keeping?'

'She went down to the chapel to say a prayer,' Johnny ground out through the side of his mouth. 'Three hours ago!' he ended in a thunderclap.

'Three hours ago?' she said incredulously, leaning her elbow on the sideboard and looking a million times prettier than Johnny had ever seen her look, in her tight-fitting coat and skirt with the little wisps of goldy-brown hair straying from under the cocky hat. 'Wisha, Johnny, I don't know would I like an old one like that around the house at all. Sure, she'd have you persecuted with piety.'

'Hell to your soul, woman!' roared Johnny, stopping dead in his bearlike shamble about the room. 'Sure, the chapel is shut since ten!'

'And this her first night here and all!' exclaimed the doctor. 'She must have drink taken. Did you try the guards' barracks?'

'Drink?' said Johnny unsuspectingly. 'Where the hell would she get drink? She had nothing here only a couple of glasses of wine to her supper.'

'And do you tell me she had wine to her supper?' asked the doctor. 'Begor, 'tisn't everyone can have that, Johnny. So what happened then?'

'What happened then was she said she wanted to go to the chapel,' shouted Johnny, well aware of how unconvincing it sounded.

'And after having wine and everything?' said the doctor incredulously. 'Ah, Johnny, you must take me for a great gom entirely. You're not telling me the whole story at all, Johnny. Go on now, and tell us what did you do to the unfortunate girl to drive her out of a night like this.'

'Me?' Johnny cried indignantly. 'I done nothing to her.'

'Not as much as a squeeze?'

'Not as much as a what?' he boomed in bellowing fury. 'What do you take me for? Go out of my sight, you malicious, wicked, mocking jade! I have no time to waste on the likes of you.'

'What do I take you for?' retorted the doctor. 'And what were the pair of ye doing with sofas and cushions and whiskey and wine? How do I know what you'd do if you had a few drinks in you? Maybe you'd be just as lively as the rest of them. Is she living here with you, Johnny?' she asked with interest.

'Where else would she live?' growled Johnny.

'And ye not married or anything!' the doctor said reproachfully. ''Twouldn't be down to the priest she went to ease her conscience about it?'

'What in God's name do you mean, woman?' Johnny asked, brought to a dead halt like a wild horse the trainer has exhausted.

'Wisha, Johnny, are you ever going to get a bit of sense?' she continued pityingly. 'At your age oughtn't you know damn well that in a town like this you couldn't bring a girl just out of school to live with you?'

'But, God above!' Johnny said in an indignant whisper, his hands clasped, his face gone white. 'I meant no harm to the girl.'

'And how do you expect her to know?' asked the doctor.

'How would a little gom like that know that 'twasn't the White Slave traders had hold of her? She's up in my digs now, if you want to know, doing hysterics on the landlady. At least she was when I left. She's probably doped or dead by now, because I gave her enough to quieten a dancehall.'

'But why – why did she go to your house?'

'Because the priest was out at a party, and you mentioned my name to her – thanks for the reference! And now give us her things and let us go home to our bed. God knows, Johnny Desmond, you should have more sense!'

As she was driving away she suddenly put her head out of the window.

'Johnny!' she called.

'What is it now?' Johnny asked irritably, pulling up the collar of his coat and running across the pavement to her.

'Tell us, Johnny,' she said innocently, 'why haven't you a few pictures on the walls?'

'Ask my arse!' hissed Johnny malevolently and rushed back to shelter.

'Johnny!' she called again. 'Aren't you going to kiss and be friends?'

'Kiss my arse!' shouted Johnny as he banged the door.

3

Next day about lunchtime he dropped into the new shop. He had deliberately left it alone till then. Everything inside seemed to be going grand. The new chemist was serving a customer and she turned to give him a smile like a sunbeam. It filled his heart with bitterness. The devil a hair astray on her, and the night she had given him! He waited till the customer left and then called her into the parlour. She stopped to give a few instructions to the assistant and followed him.

'You're comfortable where you are?' he asked gruffly.

'Oh, grand, Mr Desmond, thanks,' she replied and had the grace to blush.

' 'Twas a mistake about last night,' he said awkwardly, lifting his cap and scratching his head. ' 'Twas my fault. I blame myself a lot for it. It should have occurred to me. But I'll make it up on the wages.'

'Oh, it's all right,' she said. ''Tis only on Daddy's account. He'd kill me.'

'I wouldn't wish for a thousand pounds you'd think anything wrong was intended,' Johnny said in a choking voice. 'If you saw Father Ring last night instead of the – person you did see,' (the doctor's name stuck in his gullet) 'he'd tell you. If I made a mistake 'twas because the likes of it would never cross my mind. I was never in all my days mixed up in work like that.'

'Ah, there's no reason for you to apologize,' she said earnestly. 'It was my own fault. I see now I was foolish. The doctor told me.'

'It might be for the best,' said Johnny. He pulled a chair closer to him, rested his foot on it, his elbow on his knee, and then joined his hands as he studied her. 'There's a certain thing I was going to say,' he said thickly. 'I wasn't going to say it in a hurry. I wanted to give you time to look round you and see what sort of man I am and what sort of home I have. I'm afraid of no inquiry. I have nothing to hide. That's the sort I am. But,' he went on, growing purple at the very thought of the doctor and her gibing tongue, 'after the people you might see and the things you might hear, I'd sooner say it now. Here's the house and here's the man!'

'It's a lovely house, isn't it?' she said admiringly.

'It ought to be,' he said complacently. 'It cost two thousand eight hundred pounds. You might notice I left the pictures on one side. It seems what suits one doesn't suit all. You could choose the pictures yourself.'

'You want me to choose the pictures, Mr Desmond?' she asked in bewilderment.

'I want you to choose myself, girl,' Johnny said passionately, kicking the chair to the other side of the room. 'That was why I picked you out in Dublin. I was sure you were the right girl for me.'

'Oh, I couldn't do that, Mr Desmond,' she said in alarm, backing away from him.

'Why couldn't you?'

'Daddy would never allow it.'

'I'd talk to your father.'

'Oh, I'd rather you didn't,' she said in panic. 'You have no idea, the sort of man he is. He'd blame it all on me. Besides, I have no inclination for marriage.'

'Don't say no till you have time to look round you,' Johnny advised her shrewdly. 'You'll see what people will say about me. I'd make you a good husband. My money is safe, and when I die I'll leave you the richest woman in these parts. And, mind,' he added, pointing a finger at her, 'I'd make no conditions. I saw too much of the dead man's meanness. If you wanted to marry again there would be nothing to stop you.'

She was really frightened now. She had never seen anyone like this before, and was half afraid that by sheer will-power Johnny would make her marry him in spite of herself.

'Oh, I couldn't, I couldn't really,' she said desperately. 'I'd sooner not get married at all, but if I have to, I'll have to marry the fellow I'm going with. I'm not sure that he's suitable at all; I don't think he has the right attitude – I have terrible doubts about him sometimes – but I could never think of anyone else.'

'Think over it,' Johnny said hopelessly. 'You might change.'

But he knew she wouldn't. Women were like that. It was a lingo he couldn't speak, and it was too late for him to learn. His fortune and his beautiful house and his furniture were in a different language altogether, a language this chit of a girl wouldn't understand for another thirty years, if she ever learned it at all.

He died less than a year later and the story goes in town that the chagrin killed him. The Foxy Desmonds of the Glen blew the labours of a lifetime on fur coats and motor-cars. Only the doctor believes that it was all on her account and that what Johnny really died of was a broken heart. Women are great on broken hearts.

Orphans

Hilda Redmond lived across the road from us in Cork. She was a slight, fresh-complexioned woman with a long, thin face, and a nervous, eager, laughing manner. Her husband was tall and big-built, good-looking but morose; a man who you felt could never have been exactly gay. He was very attached to their two children, two little girls with whom you saw him walking out in the country every Sunday afternoon, each holding a hand, while he bowed to answer their questions. Though we became casually friendly he never spoke to me about Hilda, except once to make fun of her sense of her own inadequacy. As for Hilda, she is the sort of girl who will always feel inadequate.

She had been brought up in a town in the North of Ireland, a small, black, bitter little seaside town, rent by politics and religion. She was an only child, earnest and rather humourless, the sort of girl who in other circumstances would probably have devoted herself to some cause, and who, since there was no cause, took it out in piety. She was always a devout girl, conscientious to a fault.

One evening she and another girl were out walking when they were accosted by two soldiers. She had always been warned to shun soldiers, but she had also been warned to be polite, and Hilda couldn't see for the life of her how you could do the one and at the same time the other. Her companion, who was a flighty girl anyway, was no help to her. The result might have been foreseen. Hilda was seen home by a young soldier who insisted on addressing her by her first name. He was a tall lad with a very bony face and high cheekbones, and he had a nice way of smiling with a front tooth that wasn't there.

Hilda was really desperate because she felt it would be most uncivil of her not to ask him in. She did so, and he accepted

without a trace of embarrassment. There was something almost
sinister to her in his free and easy air. He greeted her parents
too as if they were old friends, though her father started every
time he heard her called 'Hilda'. Being reserved and quiet
people, they were even more scared of him than she was, but he
was a charmer, a bit of a playboy, and he knew that he had
only to make them laugh to break down their reserve.

He sat on a low chair by the fire and picked up the poker –
a curious, instinctive gesture she often noticed later – and told
them about himself. He had been brought up in a Cork orphanage with his younger brother, Larry, and he described how his
mother, when she fell ill, had brought them to the orphanage
door and left them with a monk. As she went back down the
avenue, Larry had run screaming after her, demanding to be
taken home. 'Sure, I have no home now, childeen,' she had
said. For close on a year, Larry, against all the rules had
climbed into Jim's bed and Jim had been punished for it. He
told it lightly, almost humorously, as though it were just another good story, but the Cramers did not smile. Hilda saw
tears in her mother's eyes. She never forgot the picture of him
that first evening, sitting across the fireplace from her, looking
up with wide, unblinking eyes as he told them about his youth
in a quiet, husky voice that was rough but well bred.

He did not leave without an invitation to come back, and
he took advantage of this to the point of bad manners, but
somehow they did not resent it from him. He took the house
for his own as if he were some stray pup who had adopted it;
came at every free hour, to shave or change or talk to Hilda's
parents, or go walking with her, and it never seemed to matter
much to him which of these he did. He was more like a brother
than a sweetheart, and afterwards it occurred to her that it
might have been the family he cared for rather than herself in
particular. There were things about him that bothered her. He
retained something of the stray pup or the tame bird; a trace
of wildness and a weakness for tangents. He seemed to have no
shyness and no sense of the value of money (which shocked the
Cramers who were all thrifty) and if he saw some little present
that might conceivably amuse her mother or herself, he had to

buy it, even if he had to borrow the money from her to do it. Yet even this had its pleasant side because they enjoyed the slight feeling of dissipation it gave them.

When he asked her to marry him, Hilda admitted in her candid way that she liked him better than any other fellow she knew (her acquaintance with 'fellows' was not extensive), but that she would have to be said by her parents. They, of course, were disappointingly cautious. They liked Jim, as they would have liked any young man who loved their daughter but did not want to separate her from them, and they agreed that if in twelve months' time he and Hilda still cared as much for one another they would think better of it, but in the meantime, there was the war, and Hilda was so young, and – though they did not say it to Jim – they would not like her to be left a widow so early in life.

Because Jim was easygoing and had adopted them even more than they had adopted him he could not insist too much. At the same time, Hilda knew he had set his heart on marrying her, and he even talked in his wild way of deserting and going back to Southern Ireland where he could not be reached.

Soon after that he was killed, and his death came as a real blow to Hilda. She had not realized how fond of him she was. It was her first brush with tragedy, and she was the stuff of which tragedy is made. Her parents were not. Though they felt Jim's death as a personal loss, they could scarcely avoid feeling that they had done the right thing by her. Hilda was now convinced that she had done the wrong thing; that Jim, who had never known a home, had wanted to make one with her, and that, through weakness of character, she had deprived him of the chance. She was not fair to herself, but she was an earnest girl and earnest people are rarely fair to themselves.

At the same time, having been brought up to a rigid code, she felt she must not let her parents know that she blamed them or that Jim's death had changed her in any way. A few months after, she started to walk out again, this time with a young mechanic called Jack Giltinan. Jack was a small, plump, full-flavoured man who was going bald at an early age. He had a small, round, wrinkled face and tiny, brown, twinkling eyes.

There was something birdlike about Jack, in his quickness and lightness, the cock of his eye and the angle of his head. Hilda, who in her earnestness was intent on not pretending to things she didn't feel, thought it her duty to tell him all about Jim and warn him that she could never feel quite the same about anyone else, but this didn't seem to worry Jack at all. He even seemed pleased with it.

'But it's only natural, Hilda,' he said in his excitable, anxious way. 'After all, it happened, and you can't make it happen different now.'

'It's only that I wouldn't like to pretend anything, Jack,' she explained regretfully.

'Och, what need is there for pretending?' he asked, fluttering in an agony of concern. 'If you were the sort to forget a fellow a week after he was killed, that would be something to pretend about. No man minds things like that. A man likes a girl to be sincere – yes, sincere,' he added, as though he had only just made up the word. 'It's foolish, don't you know, to be jealous of that sort of thing as if there wasn't love enough in the world for all of us. My goodness, it's crazy!'

So they talked of Jim as though he had been an old friend, wondered what would have happened to him, and wondered too about his younger brother, Larry. 'I must say I'd like to see that boy,' Jack said thoughtfully. 'I think if I did maybe I'd understand his brother better. Sometimes I can't help wondering about Jim, the way you describe him. You won't mind my saying it, Hilda – I wonder was he steady.'

She did not mind his saying it; she knew he liked people to be 'steady' as he liked them to be 'sincere', and grew as embarrassed as a girl when he noticed examples of 'unsteadiness' among his friends. Before she agreed to marry him, she realized that, apparently without wanting to do it, he had changed her attitude to Jim's death, and made it seem no longer a nightmare but a valuable experience that had deepened her own character.

2

Then one evening when she came home from work her mother met her at the door, her hand to her cheek.

'Guess who's here!' she whispered dramatically. Mrs Cramer was a woman who loved a bit of drama if only she could be sure where the dramatic interest lay.

'Who's that, Mum?' asked Hilda who was always amused by her mother's hushed histrionics.

'Someone you were wondering about,' whispered her mother, the emphasis hovering unsteadily between grief and delight.

'I can't guess,' said Hilda with a ringing laugh.

'Jim's brother.'

'Oh, dear!' said Hilda, and it was only later that she remembered what her first reaction had been.

When she went down the steps to the snug little kitchen a tall officer rose slowly from his seat by the fire. She did not need to search for the resemblance to Jim though his face was broader and gloomier and his manners had none of his brother's ease and self-confidence. Suddenly she found herself weeping quietly.

'Och, Larry,' she said, taking his hand in her two, 'and it was only two nights ago that Jack and myself were wondering what happened to you!'

'Quite a lot,' he muttered in confusion. 'I was in Egypt most of the time.'

'And where are you staying now, Larry?'

'At the hotel. I spent the last ten days in the orphanage ... They let us take our holidays there,' he added by way of explanation. 'Anyway I wanted to see it again.'

She noticed that he did not explain what he was doing in the North of Ireland. It could, of course, mean that he was on special duty, but it left her with a feeling of uneasiness. It came over her several times when she looked up and saw him sitting there, in Jim's old place. There was something about the way in which both of them had intruded unexpectedly on the household.

Her father, eager to learn about the war, monopolized him over supper, and afterwards Jack came in. 'Jack and I are engaged,' Hilda said apologetically. She didn't know what made her say that either. Larry grinned in a friendly way and congratulated them. 'We must celebrate that,' he said firmly and brought a bottle of whiskey from his topcoat in the hall. Her father and Jack each took a glass and then laid off but Larry continued to drink steadily.

'It's only for my health,' he explained with an anxious look.

'Why, Larry?' Hilda broke in innocently. 'Is your health not good?'

Then her father and Jack laughed and she saw that she had said the wrong thing as usual, but she didn't mind because she saw that Larry enjoyed a joke exactly like Jim though his style was different. With Jim you could always tell when he was joking.

Jack, who had an early start at the machine shop, left early and Hilda accompanied him to the door to say goodnight. She could see he was impressed by Larry. As he put on his overcoat in his hasty, absent-minded way he murmured: 'That's a real nice fellow, Hilda. He's been through a hell of a lot though. More than he lets on. He needs a good rest.'

Larry stayed till close on midnight, and she had the feeling that he would have stayed all night if given the chance. He was like Jim in that too. She guided him through the blackout to his hotel, past the narrow streets that let through the wind and the noise of the sea.

'When do you have to go back, Larry?' she asked.

'I still have a few days' leave,' he replied. 'I thought I might spend them here if I wasn't in your way.'

'Och, Larry, how could you be in our way?' she asked in distress.

'I went to Cork to see the old spots where Jim and myself used to go,' he went on.

'I don't know that there's many places here that Jim used to go,' she said, responding to the idea rather than the words he had used. 'He wasn't here all that long, you know. He was fond of Inish, though. If you liked I could take you there to-morrow. Jack has a Union meeting so he won't be free.'

They agreed on this, but all the same she was disturbed. Jim's death which had sunk into the background of her thoughts, was now very much to the fore again, and she found the hurt no less. Besides, she had the feeling that he and Larry had both entered her life without her consent, had scraped at her door like a stray dog or been blown in from the storm like a wild bird.

She felt it even more next day in Inish, the seaside town that Jim had liked. Jim had always loved crowds and the sea, un-like Jack who preferred country roads and cross-country walks; and she realized that since Jim's death she had not visited the place.

'I suppose we avoid it because we don't want to think,' she said as they walked up the little promenade over the beach.

'I suppose so,' he said doubtfully. 'It's different with me.'

'But Larry,' she said timidly, 'why do you do it if it upsets you?'

'I didn't say it upset me,' he replied with a frown. 'I like thinking of Jim. I dare say that's why I wanted to meet you and your family. He said so much about you.'

'Oh, I know what you mean,' she cried hastily, feeling a hint of reproach in his words. 'I told Jack I could never feel the same about anyone again . . . It's not that I wasn't fond of Jim, Larry,' she added earnestly. 'Jack can tell you that. But we have to live just the same, don't you think? It's not fair to other people if we don't. We have to think of them too.'

'Oh, I wasn't criticizing you,' he said hastily with a blush. 'You have your father and mother to think of, but I never had anyone, only Jim. The monks wanted me to take a job in Cork, but I joined the army, hoping I could get to be with him. Maybe if I had he'd still be alive.'

'Och, Larry, that's a thing we can't know,' she sighed. They had passed the promenade and were walking out along the little pier to the lighthouse. They sat on a heap of boulders and looked across the channel in the evening light. She turned on him suddenly almost in desperation. Hilda had the sudden forthrightness of very shy people. 'You want to get yourself killed, Larry, don't you?' she asked gently.

The question seemed to startle him. He paused before answering.

'I suppose there's something in that,' he replied, almost in a growl. 'I never thought of it that way, but I suppose that's what I want.'

'But you shouldn't, Larry,' she said, pleading with him. 'It's wrong. Really, it's wrong. No matter how hard it is, we must try and live.'

Then he said something in a very low voice, full of shame and anger, which she just barely caught. 'It's different when you have someone to live for. I could do it if I had you.'

Then she knew that this was what she had been dreading the whole time since her mother told her he was in the house. This was what had really brought him here. He had come here, as he had gone to Cork, to say goodbye to her as to another part of his brother, but all the time with the hope that through her he might again make contact with the living world. That was the thing he and Jim had in common; that demand of the lost for admission, that scraping on the locked door late at night. And she knew that this was why she had told him at once that she was engaged to Jack.

'But that's impossible, Larry,' she whispered in consternation. 'I told you already that I was engaged.'

He went on talking as though he had not heard her, without looking at her, almost as though he were talking to himself. He still had the same resentful expression and angry tone, as though he felt humiliated by it.

'I know I drink too much. Brother Murphy in the orphanage said he'd knock me down next time I let the kids see me like that. But that's only since Jim died. I could give that up. I know I could. I'm not boasting.'

'Och, it's not the drink, Larry,' she cried in distress. 'Not that I like it – I never did, in anyone – but that's not the reason. I suffered too, Larry; you mightn't think it, but I did, and Jack helped me when I was feeling wretched, much the way you are now. How could I upset him?'

'I know that, Hilda,' he said, regaining control of himself. 'I wasn't really expecting you to give him up. I know he's a fine man. I only wanted you to know.'

They drove back over the hills in the dusk, Larry embarrassed like a naughty child and Hilda almost hysterical. When they separated he asked meekly if he could meet her again next day, and she replied at once that she thought it better he shouldn't. Then, as she heard the fear make her voice harsh, she changed and suggested that they meet again the evening after, before he left.

'But you won't mind if I ask you not to say a thing like that to me again?' she asked urgently.

'No, Hilda, I won't ask you again,' he replied, and she knew he had far less hope of influencing her than she had fear of being influenced.

3

Next evening Jack and she went for their favourite walk over the hills to the main road. It was such a relief to be with him again that she told him the whole story. To her astonishment, he seemed very much put out. Somehow, after her previous experience with him she had grown to think of him as a rock of sense. He stood in the roadway and looked at her, his head cocked like a bird's and a look of dismay on his round russet face.

'But you're not thinking of marrying him, are you?' he asked anxiously.

'No, Jack, of course not,' she replied almost impatiently. 'I asked him not to mention it again and he won't. I know he won't. I'm sure Larry is a wee bit ashamed of himself already. Why do you ask?'

'Because I don't like it, that's all,' Jack said, shaking his head anxiously. He pulled at a bough till it snapped and as they walked on he began to strip it of its leaves. 'I suppose it's the way I'm jealous,' he added with his usual frankness. 'Of course, I am too, but it's not only that. It's unhealthy, Hilda. That's how I feel and that's not all jealousy. No, no, no,' he went on, shaking his head again as though he were reassuring himself of his own frankness. 'His brother is dead, and he can't bring him back to life. And that's not the whole story, Hilda. He likes thinking of his brother *because* he's dead. The dead have no minds of their own. You can't fight with the dead. He won't give up the drink. I watched the way he lowered it. That fellow will go dippy if he's not careful.'

'But I thought you said you liked him, Jack,' she protested.

'Och, aye, I like him all right,' he went on, worrying away at the subject like a little terrier. 'Underneath he's probably good stuff. But I can't stand this clinging to the past, to what can't be remedied. It's not healthy, I tell you. You'd want to mind what you said to him, Hilda.'

'But I said nothing to him, Jack. Only what I told you. And I couldn't say more than that.'

'No, no, no, Hilda,' he said comfortingly. 'I know you'd always do the right thing. It's only that I can't help worrying about you. I was hoping you were over this shock, and now it all seems to be beginning again.'

As usual she saw he was right. It was beginning again, and something about it was wrong. She saw that Larry was attracted to her by the feeling of his brother about her, and this was not right. And as a result of her talk with Jack, the whole situation had become more menacing, for while it was easy enough to say no to Larry out of consideration for Jack, her talk with him had made it clear to her that though beside Larry he gave an impression of lightness, physical and mental, he was really in every way the stronger man. She had noticed even in the way he pulled himself up for a word, probing his own motives, that however little there might be of him, he was in complete control of it. What there was of him was all of a piece, all 'steady', but in Larry as in Jim, under the apparent manliness and real courage there was a quaking bog of emotion that probably went back to their childhood loss. Jim, the more instinctive of the two, would have married and made a home for himself to replace the one he had lost, but Larry wanted a brother as well as a wife – a brother probably more than a wife – and this was something he could only find in her.

'What's wrong, dear?' her mother asked her over breakfast next morning. 'Did something upset you?'

'Och, it's only Larry,' Hilda said with an excuse for a smile. 'He asked me to marry him.'

'Larry did?' cried her mother, feeling that the statement required a dramatic response but uncertain what form it should take. 'There's a surprise for you!' she exclaimed, clasping her hands in case the expected response should be joyous. 'He didn't take long,' she added doubtfully, to protect her flank.

'Oh, it's nothing,' Hilda said. 'Only nice feeling. He knows how fond we were of Jim. But it brought things back.'

'He shouldn't do a thing like that though,' her mother said, realizing at last what form her response should take. 'What did you say?'

'Oh, only that I was engaged to Jack,' Hilda said wearily, repeating an argument that had begun to lose its force from the moment she knew that she needed Jack more than he needed her. Then she said something that surprised herself almost as much as it did her mother.

'Would Dad and you mind if I did marry him, Mum?'

Her mother, she could see, did not know what to say. She wiped her hands on her apron.

'Did you fight with Jack?' she asked in distress.

'Och, no, Mum, nothing like that!' Hilda exclaimed. 'I'd never hope to find a better man than Jack.'

'Of course I couldn't say, dear,' said her mother, seeing that Hilda would not further develop her relations with Jack. 'I suppose it's a matter for yourself. We wouldn't know how you felt.'

'I don't know myself how I feel,' Hilda said, shaking her head with a feeble smile. 'Jack says 'tis unhealthy, that 'tis wrong to keep thinking of the dead.'

'We can't help thinking of the dead, child,' her mother retorted with sudden sternness. 'And the older we grow the more we have to think of them. But this has nothing to do with Jim. It's not Jim you'd be marrying but Larry.'

'Oh, dear!' sighed Hilda. 'If only it was as easy as that to separate them!'

By that time she had a nervous headache and lay down instead of going to work. She was so scared by the prospect of her meeting with Larry that she almost asked her mother to go to the hotel and put him off. Yet when she opened the front door that evening and saw him on the steps with the permanent slight stoop of a man who is a couple of inches too tall, she was so relieved that she suddenly found herself becoming joyous and even silly. She giggled and gasped like a schoolgirl and her mother, observing the change in her manner, became warmer in her own.

'Where will we go, Larry?' she asked almost flirtatiously as they went down the little street. 'As it's your last night we should go somewhere nice.'

'It was nice enough where we went the last time,' he said.

'No, Larry,' she said with sudden determination. 'We won't go where we went the last time. It's wrong. Jack says it and I agree. You can't like me just because I was Jim's girl, and I can't like you because you're Jim's brother. We have our own lives to live.'

As she said it she almost gasped because she realized that she had already made her choice. Jack, of course, was right, and it was unhealthy as he said, but she felt she could deal with that. Now it was only as Jim's girl, the one living link with his brother, and beyond that with a mother and home he had forgotten, that Larry could care for her, and it might be years before he came to like her for what she was, but she preferred it that way. For the second time she had heard the call in the night, the scraping at the back door, and this time she would not disregard it. Like all earnest people, Hilda went through life looking for a cause, and now he was her cause, and she would serve him the best way she knew.

The Babes in the Wood

Whenever Mrs Early made Terry put on his best trousers and gansey he knew his aunt must be coming. She didn't come half often enough to suit Terry, but when she did it was great gas. Terry's mother was dead and he lived with Mrs Early and her son, Billy. Mrs Early was a rough, deaf, scolding old woman, doubled up with rheumatics, who'd give you a clout as quick as she'd look at you, but Billy was good gas too.

This particular Sunday morning Billy was scraping his chin frantically and cursing the bloody old razor while the bell was ringing up the valley for Mass, when Terry's aunt arrived. She came into the dark little cottage eagerly, her big rosy face toasted with sunshine and her hand out in greeting.

'Hello, Billy,' she cried in a loud, laughing voice, 'late for Mass again?'

'Let me alone, Miss Conners,' stuttered Billy, turning his lathered face to her from the mirror. 'I think my mother shaves on the sly.'

'And how's Mrs Early?' cried Terry's aunt, kissing the old woman and then fumbling at the strap of her knapsack in her excitable way. Everything about his aunt was excitable and high-powered; the words tumbled out of her so fast that sometimes she became incoherent.

'Look, I brought you a couple of things – no, they're fags for Billy' – ('God bless you, Miss Conners,' from Billy) – 'this is for you, and here are a few things for the dinner.'

'And what did you bring me, Auntie?' Terry asked.

'Oh, Terry,' she cried in consternation, 'I forgot about you.'

'You didn't.'

'I did, Terry,' she said tragically. 'I swear I did. Or did I? The bird told me something. What was it he said?'

'What sort of bird was it?' asked Terry. 'A thrush?'

'A big grey fellow?'

'That's the old thrush all right. He sings in our back yard.'

'And what was that he told me to bring you?'

'A boat!' shouted Terry.

It was a boat.

After dinner the pair of them went up the wood for a walk. His aunt had a long, swinging stride that made her hard to keep up with, but she was great gas and Terry wished she'd come to see him oftener. When she did he tried his hardest to be grown-up. All the morning he had been reminding himself: 'Terry, remember you're not a baby any longer. You're nine now, you know.' He wasn't nine, of course; he was still only five and fat, but nine, the age of his girlfriend Florrie, was the one he liked pretending to be. When you were nine you understood everything. There were still things Terry did not understand.

When they reached the top of the hill his aunt threw herself on her back with her knees in the air and her hands under her head. She liked to toast herself like that. She liked walking; her legs were always bare; she usually wore a tweed skirt and a pullover. Today she wore black glasses, and when Terry looked through them he saw everything dark; the wooded hills at the other side of the valley and the buses and cars crawling between the rocks at their feet, and, still farther down, the railway track and the river. She promised him a pair for himself next time she came, a small pair to fit him, and he could scarcely bear the thought of having to wait so long for them.

'When will you come again, Auntie?' he asked. 'Next Sunday?'

'I might,' she said and rolled on her belly, propped her head on her hands, and sucked a straw as she laughed at him. 'Why? Do you like it when I come?'

'I love it.'

'Would you like to come and live with me altogether, Terry?'

'Oh, Jay, I would.'

'Are you sure now?' she said, half ragging him. 'You're sure you wouldn't be lonely after Mrs Early or Billy or Florrie?'

'I wouldn't, Auntie, honest,' he said tensely. 'When will you bring me?'

'I don't know yet,' she said. 'It might be sooner than you think.'

'Where would you bring me? Up to town?'

'If I tell you where,' she whispered, bending closer, 'will you swear a terrible oath not to tell anybody?'

'I will.'

'Not even Florrie?'

'Not even Florrie.'

'That you might be killed stone dead?' she added in a bloodcurdling tone.

'That I might be killed stone dead!'

'Well, there's a nice man over from England who wants to marry me and bring me back with him. Of course, I said I couldn't come without you and he said he'd bring you as well ... Wouldn't that be gorgeous?' she ended, clapping her hands.

''Twould,' said Terry, clapping his hands in imitation. 'Where's England?'

'Oh, a long way off,' she said, pointing up the valley. 'Beyond where the railway ends. We'd have to get a big boat to take us there.'

'Chrisht!' said Terry, repeating what Billy said whenever something occurred too great for his imagination to grasp, a fairly common event. He was afraid his aunt, like Mrs Early, would give him a wallop for it, but she only laughed. 'What sort of a place is England, Auntie?' he went on.

'Oh, a grand place,' said his aunt in her loud, enthusiastic way. 'The three of us would live in a big house of our own with lights that went off and on, and hot water in the taps, and every morning I'd take you to school on your bike.'

'Would I have a bike of my own?' Terry asked incredulously.

'You would, Terry, a two-wheeled one. And on a fine day like this we'd sit in the park – you know, a place like the garden of the big house where Billy works, with trees and flowers and a pond in the middle to sail boats in.'

'And would we have a park of our own, too?'

'Not our own; there'd be other people as well; boys and girls you could play with. And you could be sailing your boat and I'd be reading a book, and then we'd go back home to tea and I'd bath you and tell you a story in bed. Wouldn't it be massive, Terry?'

'What sort of story would you tell me?' he asked cautiously. 'Tell us one now.'

So she took off her black spectacles and, hugging her knees, told him the story of the Three Bears and was so carried away that she acted it, growling and wailing and creeping on all fours with her hair over her eyes till Terry screamed with fright and pleasure. She was really great gas.

2

Next day Florrie came to the cottage for him. Florrie lived in the village so she had to come a mile through the woods to see him, but she delighted in seeing him and Mrs Early encouraged her. 'Your young lady' she called her and Florrie blushed with pleasure. Florrie lived with Miss Clancy in the post office and was very nicely behaved; everyone admitted that. She was tall and thin, with jet-black hair, a long ivory face, and a hook nose.

'Terry!' bawled Mrs Early. 'Your young lady is here for you,' and Terry came rushing from the back of the cottage with his new boat.

'Where did you get that, Terry?' Florrie asked, opening her eyes wide at the sight of it.

'My auntie,' said Terry. 'Isn't it grand?'

'I suppose 'tis all right,' said Florrie, showing her teeth in a smile which indicated that she thought him a bit of a baby for making so much of a toy boat.

Now, that was one great weakness in Florrie, and Terry regretted it because he really was very fond of her. She was gentle, she was generous, she always took his part; she told creepy stories so well that she even frightened herself and was scared of going back through the woods alone, but she was jealous. Whenever she had anything, even if it was only a

raggy doll, she made it out to be one of the seven wonders of
the world, but let anyone else have a thing, no matter how
valuable, and she pretended it didn't even interest her. It was
the same now.

'Will you come up to the big house for a pennorth of goosegogs?' she asked.

'We'll go down the river with this one first,' insisted Terry,
who knew he could always override her wishes when he chose.

'But these are grand goosegogs,' she said eagerly, and again
you'd think no one in the world but herself could even have a
gooseberry. 'They're that size. Miss Clancy gave me the
penny.'

'We'll go down the river first,' Terry said cantankerously.
'Ah, boy, wait till you see this one sail – sssss!'

She gave in as she always did when Terry showed himself
headstrong, and grumbled as she always did when she had
given in. She said it would be too late; that Jerry, the under-
gardener, who was their friend, would be gone and that Mr
Scott, the head gardener, would only give them a handful, and
not even ripe ones. She was terrible like that, an awful old
worrier.

When they reached the riverbank they tied up their clothes
and went in. The river was deep enough, and under the trees it
ran beautifully clear over a complete pavement of small, brown,
smoothly rounded stones. The current was swift, and the little
sailing-boat was tossed on its side and spun dizzily round and
round before it stuck in the bank. Florrie tired of this sport
sooner than Terry did. She sat on the bank with her hands under her bottom, trailing her toes in the river, and looked at the
boat with growing disillusionment.

'God knows, 'tisn't much of a thing to lose a pennorth of
goosegogs over,' she said bitterly.

'What's wrong with it?' Terry asked indignantly. ''Tis a
fine boat.'

'A wonder it wouldn't sail properly so,' she said with an accusing, schoolmarmish air.

'How could it when the water is too fast for it?' shouted
Terry.

'That's a good one,' she retorted in pretended grown-up amusement. ' 'Tis the first time we ever heard of water being too fast for a boat.' That was another very aggravating thing about her – her calm assumption that only what she knew was knowledge. ' 'Tis only a cheap old boat.'

' 'Tisn't a cheap old boat,' Terry cried indignantly. 'My aunt gave it to me.'

'She never gives anyone anything only cheap old things,' Florrie replied with the coolness that always maddened other children. 'She gets them cost price in the shop where she works. Everyone knows that.'

'Because you're jealous,' he cried, throwing at her the taunt the village children threw whenever she enraged them with her supercilious airs.

'That's a good one too,' she said in a quiet voice, while her long thin face maintained its air of amusement. 'I suppose you'll tell us now what we're jealous of?'

'Because Auntie brings me things and no one ever brings you anything.'

'She's mad about you,' Florrie said ironically.

'She is mad about me.'

'A wonder she would bring you to live with her so.'

'She's going to,' said Terry, forgetting his promise in his rage and triumph.

'She is, I hear!' Florrie said mockingly. 'Who told you that?'

'She did; Auntie.'

'Don't mind her at all, little boy,' Florrie said severely. 'She lives with her mother, and her mother wouldn't let you live with her.'

'Well, she's not going to live with her any more,' Terry said, knowing he had the better of her at last. 'She's going to get married.'

'Who is she going to get married to?' Florrie asked casually, but Terry could see she was impressed.

'A man in England, and I'm going to live with them. So there!'

'In England?' Florrie repeated, and Terry saw he had really knocked the stuffing out of her this time. Florrie had no one to bring her to England, and the jealousy was driving her mad. 'And I suppose you're going?' she asked bitterly.

'I am going,' Terry said, wild with excitement to see her overthrown; the grand lady who for all her airs had no one to bring her to England with them. 'And I'm getting a bike of my own. So now!'

'Is that what she told you?' Florrie asked with a hatred and contempt that made him more furious still.

'She's going to, she's going to,' he shouted furiously.

'Ah, she's only codding you, little boy,' Florrie said contemptuously, splashing her long legs in the water while she continued to fix him with the same dark, evil, round-eyed look, exactly like a witch in a storybook. 'Why did she send you down here at all so?'

'She didn't send me,' Terry said, stooping to fling a handful of water in her face.

'But sure, I thought everyone knew that,' she said idly, merely averting her face slightly to avoid the splashes. 'She lets on to be your aunt but we all know she's your mother.'

'She isn't,' shrieked Terry. 'My mother is dead.'

'Ah, that's only what they always tell you,' Florrie replied quietly. 'That's what they told me too, but I knew it was lies. Your mother isn't dead at all, little boy. She got into trouble with a man and her mother made her send you down here to get rid of you. The whole village knows that.'

'God will kill you stone dead for a dirty liar, Florrie Clancy,' he said and then threw himself on her and began to pummel her with his little fat fists. But he hadn't the strength, and she merely pushed him off lightly and got up on the grassy bank, flushed and triumphant, pretending to smooth down the front of her dress.

'Don't be codding yourself that you're going to England at all, little boy,' she said reprovingly. 'Sure, who'd want you? Jesus knows I'm sorry for you,' she added with mock pity, 'and I'd like to do what I could for you, but you have no sense.'

Then she went off in the direction of the wood, turning once or twice to give him her strange stare. He glared after her and danced and shrieked with hysterical rage. He had no idea what she meant, but he felt that she had got the better of him after all. 'A big, bloody brute of nine,' he said, and then began to run through the woods to the cottage, sobbing. He knew that God would kill her for the lies she had told, but if God didn't, Mrs Early would. Mrs Early was pegging up clothes on the line and peered down at him sourly.

'What ails you now didn't ail you before?' she asked.

'Florrie Clancy was telling lies,' he shrieked, his fat face black with fury. 'Big bloody brute!'

'Botheration to you and Florrie Clancy!' said Mrs Early. 'Look at the cut of you! Come here till I wipe your nose.'

'She said my aunt wasn't my aunt at all,' he cried.

'She what?' Mrs Early asked incredulously.

'She said she was my mother – Auntie that gave me the boat,' he said through his tears.

'Aha,' Mrs Early said grimly, 'let me catch her round here again and I'll toast her backside for her, and that's what she wants, the little vagabond! Whatever your mother might do, she was a decent woman, but the dear knows who that one is or where she came from.'

3

All the same it was a bad business for Terry. A very bad business! It is all very well having fights, but not when you're only five and live a mile away from the village, and there is nowhere for you to go but across the footbridge to the little railway station and the main road where you wouldn't see another kid once in a week. He'd have been very glad to make it up with Florrie, but she knew she had done wrong and that Mrs Early was only lying in wait for her to ask her what she meant.

And to make it worse, his aunt didn't come for months. When she did, she came unexpectedly and Terry had to change his clothes in a hurry because there was a car waiting for them at the station. The car made up to Terry for the disappointment (he had never been in a car before), and to crown it, they were going to the seaside, and his aunt had brought him a brand-new bucket and spade.

They crossed the river by the little wooden bridge and there in the yard of the station was a posh grey car and a tall man beside it whom Terry hadn't seen before. He was a posh-looking fellow too, with a grey hat and a nice manner, but Terry didn't pay him much attention at first. He was too interested in the car.

'This is Mr Walker, Terry,' his aunt said in her loud way. 'Shake hands with him nicely.'

'How're ye, mister?' said Terry.

'But this fellow is a blooming boxer,' Mr Walker cried, letting on to be frightened of him. 'Do you box, young Samson?' he asked.

'I do not,' said Terry, scrambling into the back of the car and climbing up on the seat. 'Hey, mister, will we go through the village?' he added.

'What do you want to go through the village for?' asked Mr Walker.

'He wants to show off,' said his aunt with a chuckle. 'Don't you, Terry?'

'I do,' said Terry.

'Sound judge!' said Mr Walker, and they drove along the main road and up through the village street just as Mass was ending, and Terry, hurling himself from side to side, shouted to all the people he knew. First they gaped, then they laughed, finally they waved back. Terry kept shouting messages but they were lost in the noise and rush of the car. 'Billy! Billy!' he screamed when he saw Billy Early outside the church. 'This is my aunt's car. We're going for a spin. I have a bucket and spade.' Florrie was standing outside the post office with her hands behind her back. Full of magnanimity and self-importance, Terry gave her a special shout and his aunt leaned out and and waved, but though Florrie looked up she let on not to recognize them. That was Florrie all out, jealous even of the car!

Terry had not seen the sea before, and it looked so queer that he decided it was probably England. It was a nice place enough but a bit on the draughty side. There were whitewashed houses all along the beach. His aunt undressed him and made him put on bright blue bathing-drawers, but when he felt the wind he shivered and sobbed and clasped himself despairingly under the armpits.

'Ah, wisha, don't be such a baby!' his aunt said crossly.

She and Mr Walker undressed too and led him by the hand to the edge of the water. His terror and misery subsided and he sat in a shallow place, letting the bright waves crumple on his shiny little belly. They were so like lemonade that he kept on tasting them, but they tasted salt. He decided that if this was England it was all right, though he would have preferred it with a park and a bicycle. There were other children making sandcastles and he decided to do the same, but after a while, to his great annoyance, Mr Walker came to help him. Terry couldn't see why, with all that sand, he wouldn't go and make castles of his own.

'Now we want a gate, don't we?' Mr Walker asked officiously.

'All right, all right, all right,' said Terry in disgust. 'Now, you go and play over there.'

'Wouldn't you like to have a daddy like me, Terry?' Mr Walker asked suddenly.

'I don't know,' replied Terry. 'I'll ask Auntie. That's the gate now.'

'I think you'd like it where I live,' said Mr Walker. 'We've much nicer places there.'

'Have you?' asked Terry with interest. 'What sort of places?'

'Oh, you know – roundabouts and swings and things like that.'

'And parks?' asked Terry.

'Yes, parks.'

'Will we go there now?' asked Terry eagerly.

'Well, we couldn't go there today; not without a boat. It's in England, you see; right at the other side of all that water.'

'Are you the man that's going to marry Auntie?' Terry asked, so flabbergasted that he lost his balance and fell.

'Now, who told you I was going to marry Auntie?' asked Mr Walker, who seemed astonished too.

'She did,' said Terry.

'Did she, by jove?' Mr Walker exclaimed with a laugh. 'Well, I think it might be a very good thing for all of us, yourself included. What else did she tell you?'

'That you'd buy me a bike,' said Terry promptly. 'Will you?'

'Sure thing,' Mr Walker said gravely. 'First thing we'll get you when you come to live with me. Is that a bargain?'

'That's a bargain,' said Terry.

'Shake,' said Mr Walker, holding out his hand.

'Shake,' replied Terry, spitting on his own.

He was content with the idea of Mr Walker as a father. He could see he'd make a good one. He had the right principles.

They had their tea on the strand and then got back late to the station. The little lamps were lit on the platform. At the other side of the valley the high hills were masked in dark trees and no light showed the position of the Earlys' cottage. Terry was tired; he didn't want to leave the car, and began to whine.

'Hurry up now, Terry,' his aunt said briskly as she lifted him out. 'Say night-night to Mr Walker.'

Terry stood in front of Mr Walker, who had got out before him, and then bowed his head.

'Aren't you going to say goodnight, old man?' Mr Walker asked in surprise.

Terry looked up at the reproach in his voice and then threw himself blindly about his knees and buried his face in his trousers. Mr Walker laughed and patted Terry's shoulder. His voice was quite different when he spoke again.

'Cheer up, Terry,' he said. 'We'll have good times yet.'

'Come along now, Terry,' his aunt said in a brisk official voice that terrified him.

'What's wrong, old man?' Mr Walker asked.

'I want to stay with you,' Terry whispered, beginning to sob. 'I don't want to stay here. I want to go back to England with you.'

'Want to come back to England with me, do you?' Mr Walker repeated. 'Well, I'm not going back tonight, Terry, but, if you ask Auntie nicely we might manage it another day.'

'It's no use stuffing up the child with ideas like that,' she said sharply.

'You seem to have done that pretty well already,' Mr Walker said quietly. 'So you see, Terry, we can't manage it tonight. We must leave it for another day. Run along with Auntie now.'

'No, no, no,' Terry shrieked, trying to evade his aunt's arms. 'She only wants to get rid of me.'

'Now, who told you that wicked nonsense, Terry?' Mr Walker said severely.

'It's true, it's true,' said Terry. 'She's not my auntie. She's my mother.'

Even as he said it he knew it was dreadful. It was what Florrie Clancy said, and she hated his auntie. He knew it even more from the silence that fell on the other two. His aunt looked down at him and her look frightened him.

'Terry,' she said with a change of tone, 'you're to come with me at once and no more of this nonsense.'

'Let him to me,' Mr Walker said shortly. 'I'll find the place.'

She did so and at once Terry stopped kicking and whining and nosed his way into Mr Walker's shoulder. He knew the Englishman was for him. Besides he was very tired. He was half asleep already. When he heard Mr Walker's step on the planks of the wooden bridge he looked up and saw the dark hillside, hooded with pines, and the river like lead in the last light. He woke again in the little dark bedroom which he shared with Billy. He was sitting on Mr Walker's knee and Mr Walker was taking off his shoes.

'My bucket,' he sighed.

'Oh, by gum, lad,' Mr Walker said, 'I'd nearly forgotten your bucket.'

4

Every Sunday after, wet or fine, Terry found his way across the footbridge and the railway station to the main road. There was a pub there, and men came up from the valley and sat on the wall outside, waiting for the coast to be clear to slip in for a drink. In case there might be any danger of having to leave them behind, Terry brought his bucket and spade as well. You never knew when you'd need things like those. He sat at the foot of the wall near the men, where he could see the buses and cars coming from both directions. Sometimes a grey car like Mr Walker's appeared from around the corner and he waddled up the road towards it, but the driver's face was always a disappointment. In the evenings when the first buses were coming back he returned to the cottage and Mrs Early scolded him for moping and whining. He blamed himself a lot because all the trouble began when he broke his word to his aunt.

One Sunday, Florrie came up the main road from the village. She went past him slowly, waiting for him to speak to her, but he wouldn't. It was all her fault, really. Then she stopped and turned to speak to him. It was clear that she knew he'd be there and had come to see him and make it up.

'Is it anyone you're waiting for, Terry?' she asked.

'Never mind,' Terry replied rudely.

'Because if you're waiting for your aunt, she's not coming,' Florrie went on gently.

Another time Terry wouldn't have entered into conversation, but now he felt so mystified that he would have spoken to anyone who could tell him what was keeping his aunt and Mr Walker. It was terrible to be only five, because nobody ever told you anything.

'How do you know?' he asked.

'Miss Clancy said it,' replied Florrie confidently. 'Miss Clancy knows everything. She hears it all in the post office. And the man with the grey car isn't coming either. He went back to England.'

Terry began to snivel softly. He had been afraid that Mr Walker wasn't really in earnest. Florrie drew closer to him and then sat on the grass bank beside him. She plucked a stalk and began to shred it in her lap.

'Why wouldn't you be said by me?' she asked reproachfully. 'You know I was always your girl and I wouldn't tell you a lie.'

'But why did Mr Walker go back to England?' he asked.

'Because your aunt wouldn't go with him.'

'She said she would.'

'Her mother wouldn't let her. He was married already. If she went with him he'd have brought you as well. You're lucky he didn't.'

'Why?'

'Because he was a Protestant,' Florrie said primly. 'Protestants have no proper religion like us.'

Terry did his best to grasp how having a proper religion made up to a fellow for the loss of a house with lights that went off and on, a park and a bicycle, but he realized he was too young. At five it was still too deep for him.

'But why doesn't Auntie come down like she always did?'

'Because she married another fellow and he wouldn't like it.'

'Why wouldn't he like it?'

'Because it wouldn't be right,' Florrie replied almost pityingly. 'Don't you see the English fellow have no proper religion, so he wouldn't mind, but the fellow she married owns the shop she works in, and Miss Clancy says 'tis surprising he married her at all, and he wouldn't like her to be coming here to see you. She'll be having proper children now, you see.'

'Aren't we proper children?'

'Ah, no, we're not,' Florrie said despondently.

'What's wrong with us?'

That was a question that Florrie had often asked herself, but she was too proud to show a small boy like Terry that she hadn't discovered the answer.

'Everything,' she sighed.

'Florrie Clancy,' shouted one of the men outside the pub, 'what are you doing to that kid?'

'I'm doing nothing to him,' she replied in a scandalized tone, starting as though from a dream. 'He shouldn't be here by himself at all. He'll get run over ... Come on home with me now, Terry,' she added, taking his hand.

'She said she'd bring me to England and give me a bike of my own,' Terry wailed as they crossed the tracks.

'She was only codding,' Florrie said confidently. Her tone changed gradually; it was becoming fuller, more scornful.

'She'll forget all about you when she has other kids. Miss Clancy says they're all the same. She says there isn't one of them worth bothering your head about, that they never think of anyone only themselves. She says my father has pots of money. If you were in with me I might marry you when you're a bit more grown-up.'

She led him up the short cut through the woods. The trees were turning all colours. Then she sat on the grass and sedately smoothed her frock about her knees.

'What are you crying for?' she asked reproachfully. 'It was all your fault. I was always your girl. Even Mrs Early said it. I always took your part when the others were against you. I wanted you not to be said by that old one and her promises, but you cared more for her and her old toys than you did for me. I told you what she was, but you wouldn't believe me, and now, look at you! If you'll swear to be always in with me I'll be your girl again. Will you?'

'I will,' said Terry.

She put her arms about him and he fell asleep, but she remained solemnly holding him, looking at him with detached and curious eyes. He was hers at last. There were no more rivals. She fell asleep too and did not notice the evening train go up the valley. It was all lit up. The evenings were drawing in.

If you have enjoyed this PAN
Book you may like to choose
your next book from the titles
listed on the following pages

Frank O'Connor

Also in PAN is the entrancing story of O'Connor's life as schoolboy, revolutionary and director of the Abbey Theatre.

Sean O'Casey

Sean O'Casey wrote his evocative and richly entertaining autobiography in six volumes over more than two decades. Each volume is essential reading for a proper appreciation of this major Irish dramatist.

Walter Macken